CENTURION JUSTICE

THE MYSTERIOUS AND EROTIC CASE OF THE ALBINO, AFRICAN, BLACK DREAD, AND JESUS' HIT MAN

RONALD A. WHITE

iUniverse, Inc.
New York   Bloomington

Centurion Justice

iUniverse books may be ordered through booksellers or by contacting:

iUniverse
1663 Liberty Drive
Bloomington, IN 47403
www.iuniverse.com
1-800-Authors (1-800-288-4677)

ISBN: 978-1-4502-3570-9 (sc)
ISBN: 978-1-4502-3571-6 (dj)
ISBN: 978-1-4502-3572-3 (ebook)

Printed in the United States of America

iUniverse rev. date: 07/09/2010

A gripping urban crime story that takes you from the grimy, sin filled, explicit streets of Jacksonville Florida to the emerald, diamond and gold streets of the Heavenly Kingdom. You walk with Centurion on his journey of crime, punishment and justice in this life and the after- life. Experience this extra ordinary story with over the top swagger, guts and glory. I dare you to call it fiction. It's guaranteed to capture your every emotion and will transform you socially, spiritually and politically as hot nasty passion, the large caliber bullet and the Cross collide. No evil deed goes unpaid. From the ghetto to glory if you do dirt Justice gone get you. Your imagination will be possessed by the sex, excitement and drama of Centurion Justice!

For your guidance and encouragement,
Special thanks and much love to
John Figaro

In Jacksonville Florida bad things are happening, the streets are watching and this is what they see. Every 24 hours a life is taken then someone pleads for forgiveness and receives it. But every now and then evil forces collide and murders are committed that even God will not forgive. Then Jesus himself rises from the Throne and calls for Justice.

In Jacksonville there is a Brother who can answer the call, hard as steel but smooth as velvet, getting paid and issuing payback, staying on his grind while keeping his women getting off. No shackles or chains can hold his lust for female flesh and love of gun play, you wouldn't think he would be called, think again. Even though Jacksonville Vice took his badge, he's fast on the trail of wild killers who took his friends life and are terrorizing the city. You know you done wrong when Jesus wants to kill you and when Jesus wants you dead Justice hunts you down; Centurion Justice.

TABLE OF CONTENTS

CHAPTER 1 – LUCKY ME

THE VIETNAMESE GIRL at Tina's Nails sat me in a pedicure chair on the end, right next to the baddest little blonde I had ever seen. I knew my life was about to change, I just didn't know how much.

I introduced myself and told her my friends call me C.J. but she and I didn't have to be so formal. She said her name was Allison Alldaway, but she might as well have said it was lips, titties and round tight ass 'cause that's all I could see. Allison was about five foot five, brown eyes and platinum blonde hair down to the roots. She had a smile like fresh milk, skin like melted gold, a blonde goddess formed from a perfect mold; wearing a peach colored blouse with straps across the front which made a futile attempt to hold her titties back and tight white straight legged jeans that she must have had help putting on. She was thick, but not fat.

Allison told me she was married to Dr. Sam Alldaway. Dr. Sammy, as he is known, is an accomplished sports injury surgeon who specializes in foot injuries. He heads the medical department for the Pro Football Team. Dr. Sammy was out of town with the football team and she was out pampering herself.

I couldn't turn my eyes away from her Marilyn Monroe shaped face and friendly outgoing personality. She was having a pedicure, but I wanted to give her a full body massage. I don't cross the line with women who got papers on them, loving her would be wrong, but she was a bad son of a gun and before my morality could take a vote I locked in on her scent and was tracking her slightest move and had decided to stick my claw into her and maul her like Tiger.

So I asked Allison if she liked lattes, told her that there is a Starbuck's across the street. She told me to skip the small talk, she liked roughneck brothers and asked if we were going together or riding in separate cars. We drove separately but I ended up in the passenger seat of her hundred thousand dollar Mercedes convertible that Dr. Sammy had bought her for Christmas. We never went into Starbucks. Instead she served up wet, sloppy, hot tongue probing kisses. I stirred up a car full of steam and panties full of cream.

After thirty minutes or so of French licking and finger sticking, it was time we consummated our relationship. She was too noticeable and I was too well-known to hang around town. We decided to go to Daytona Beach in her car and I would drive. Within a matter of minutes, I was doing ninety-five on southbound I-95. She hung onto me like a wet T-shirt the whole way.

Forty minutes later, we were pulling into the Surfside Hotel on A1A in Daytona Beach where I stopped the white Mercedes, jumped out then ran into the check-in office and told the clerk to give me an ocean side room upstairs. The clerk put a key and registration form on the desk. I placed my driver's license and a hundred dollar bill down then grabbed the key and ran out the door.

When I got back to the car, Allison was standing next to it in just her low-cut pushup bra, lace hip-hugger panties and some two inch heels. She was about a 32-20-32 and I was 'bout a jackpot hitting son of a bitch. Here "kitty kitty." Allison Alldaway was a winning hand, two pair over a full house, even if I didn't play cards I'd want to poke her.

She had no inhibitions. We took the stairs to the room and on the way she took off the bra and panties. I turned the key in the door waiting for the lock to click, but she was already on her knees trying to turn me a trick.

I stood her up and turned her around. She grabbed the door knob. Then bent her back, spread her legs and got up on her tip toes ready to serve it like Serena. I moved up close behind her with my ten and a quarter inch dick racket. Hitting her with right and left ground strokes dead in the sweet spot, but she was a player and was knocking balls back like Venus. Like two dogs stuck together we moved inside the room when the Mexican house keeper rolled her cart by and asked if we needed clean towels. We hobbled inside and I shed all my threads. Leaving nothing but raw flesh, my stomach muscles rippling like the Colorado rapids, pecks stacked up like the Egyptian pyramids, back thick and hard like the rock of Gibraltar, dick long and strong like the river Nile, rocking her whole world. No room service or Viagra needed.

We had sex with her on top, me on top and with both of us on top. While Allison kept doing that thing white women do in flipping their hair from side to side. I kept doing that thing brothers do in trying to go deeper and deeper, from the dresser to the bed, to the chair next to the bed, then the floor and on the balcony.

I was a flesh farmer plowing up new pussy and she was fertile ground yielding a creamy harvest. I stayed at it, front door, back door and the attic. Sixty nine positions and she still wasn't straight.

We proceeded to bump and grind all the nail polish off her brand new pedicure and knocked over all the chairs and tables in the room. Allison undresses quick, but she don't cum easy.

With sweat dripping from the box springs and Allison tumbling, rolling and still doing splits, I ask her if she needed to quit. She said, "Fuck that shit and hit this clit, this white girl got to have it. I'll handle the offense, you work that 'D'. You don't stop till you satisfy me!"

So I kept beating the brakes off that coochee and she kept screaming like a banshee till the hotel manager came knocking on the door and kicked me out for obscene behavior and getting rough with a kitty cat. I don't know why he put it all on me, if she didn't have the pussy I wouldn't act like a dick!

No matter, I had taken AA through the twelve climax program and she was hooked. We left the hotel then stopped about ten miles north in Ormond Beach where we had crab cakes and martinis at a seaside restaurant then walked along the boardwalk.

So I asked her what she thought about adults who try to tip out on the sly. We just met so I ain't gonna lie. I'm a Player in the game, out for pleasure, I'm not a pirate looking to steal another man's treasure.

Allison looked me dead in my eyes and said, "I'm not just good pussy, I'm a Baller baby. In case you left home and your momma didn't tell you, a man can't miss what he can't measure. I don't need no harlequin romancing, I take off my panties, you shove in your dick and afterwards we'll go dancing. So I just want you to know, some men can fill up a woman's purse and some men can fill up a woman's panties. Remember Player, everybody in the game plays a different position. Players play and Ballers ball, my word is true, you didn't pull me, I pulled you."

Right then I knew what I had, this blonde was bad! The girl got her own car, own money, own pad. I know she's not free, but she talks that shit and works that slit like a straight up 'G'.

Lord forgive me but she's honey and I'm a bee, I just hit the jackpot, lucky me, lucky me.

Allison bought a bag of weed from the young surfer boy hanging out in the parking lot. It started to rain and we had to put the top up. I drove while Allison rolled. Then she fired up a fatty and stroked my head while blowing smoke up my nose.

Now, to the best of my recollection, it may have been the fatigue of love making or the road construction going on during a light drizzle on that day, but more likely it was the five martinis and the smoke in the car from the marijuana.

Jesus! Jesus! I remember shouting as I lost control of the Mercedes coup that she insisted we ride in and I drive. Off the shoulder of the road then I overcorrected the little white sports coup with the eggshell white interior and the platinum blonde white women in the passenger seat not wearing a seat belt. It skipped once, rolled twice and hit three trees just south of Saint Augustine Florida on Interstate 95 North.

Allison Alldaway was thrown from the vehicle and killed instantly.

When the Saint John's County paramedics checked me for injuries they were amazed; a bruised knee, shin and forearm, lacerations across my abdomen from the seatbelt I was wearing and a headache.

Jesus! You sure are lucky, one paramedic stated as I sat on the grassy road side staring at the blanket covering Allison's body. Quietly I responded, "Yeah, I'm one jackpot hitting son of a bitch."

I lived, but I wasn't just anybody. I was a cop, not just any cop, but the baddest Vice Detective to walk the streets of Jacksonville Florida. I lived, but my law enforcement career was dead as I sat on the grassy road side slope thinking lucky me, lucky me.

CHAPTER 2 – ROSA

"**S**WEETHEART, PAPI COME back to bed."
Rosa's dreamy voice said as it whipped creamed over my early morning day dream.

It wasn't until I heard Rosa's voice that I realized how tight I was gripping the window frame, while grieving over Allison's death and my fall from grace. After being awaken in the night by my seventh sense, my something aint right, get ready to fight sense.

I stood in the window of the second floor apartment. Apartment 2B at 1923 River Road which sits across the street from the south river bank in Jacksonville Florida's San Marco residential district. A neighborhood of conservatives and liberals, contemporary loafs, old renovated brick, sidewalk cafes, night clubs and book stores in the midst of long established church communities. Near the Main Street Bridge that connects San Marco to downtown, it's stylish, street wise and spiritual, kind of like me.

From the window I can see a large ship carrying containers slowly passing under the bridge. As my eyes follow the ship I see a figure standing near the water's edge. It's a male but in the moonlight; it's not much more than a silhouette. His head is tilted upward as if he's watching me in the window. I leaned closer to the glass. Then he moves and walks quickly off into the shadows and down the sidewalk along River Road.

I wasn't sure how long I had been standing in the window starring into the fleeting moon as though it were a crystal ball, while looking for my future and forgiveness but only seeing the carnal x-rated movie that is my recent past as a former Jacksonville Vice Detective. A job I loved. A job I was born to do, till I went too far with Allison Alldaway.

"Papi," Rosa calls again in her juicy Hispanic voice that on occasion made me dream of sitting on a secluded beach with a handful of mango, squeezing it then licking the juice as it runs down my arm.

"Good morning," I respond while still reflecting back on my six years on the force, four with vice, where I owned the streets. At least that's what I thought.

Throughout the city each hood knew my swagger if it didn't know my name; in Floyd Circle they called me Young Ali, in Grand Park they called me Lil James Bond, downtown they called me Pretty Brown. When it came to knowing what was happening on the street, I was the breeze through the trees and the tick of the clock. I knew where, I knew when and could take a lick and keep my trigger finger clicking. I had some big bust to prove it.

Who busted the crooked cops that were robbing and killing drug dealer's and small business owner's, then using the money to buy a high and open up small businesses. These dark angels would volunteer in the church, doing their shit then drop a little something on the pulpit, till I came and gave the benediction.

Who busted the Preacher at Shilites Baptist Church for doing drugs with and raping under aged girls, baptizing them in the blood of their virginity and then using church funds to pay off their mothers. He better be glad they didn't have big brothers. Not that the church could afford it so, it's just that the price has dropped so low for a fuck and a blow. Who busted them? I did, Me, C.J., that's who.

Who busted Black Billionaires Incorporated and its network of black urban, state and religious leaders; they were a collaboration of bogus companies that siphoned money from federal and state contracts meant to boost the black community but instead funded their members' insatiable lust for power, pussy, and gambling. Living like the Black Bush's till that jigga couldn't get his money back at the track. Who busted them? me, C.J., that's who. I planted the snitches, paid the bookies for information and bugged the tricks. I was a one man criminal apprehension team. No matter how long the chase, dead or alive, I'm closing your case.

When a major corporate owner's son, who later became mayor, was rumored to have freaky sexual taste and there were pictures to prove it. Who water boarded the two paparazzi until any recollection of the events were washed from their memory. Then, I found him a trophy wife to put in place and squash the rumors. I was the shit. With an open pass to all major corporate and charity events. Untouchable and everybody knew it. I was the mayor's kick ass, find him some ass wingman and was proud of it.

I partied with the politicians while politicking for panties, a smooth street brother from the dirty south, mixing it up with the conservative beer drinking Country Club Click. Sure many of my tactics came into question as arms and legs got broken, women ended up naked and some dogs got kicked. I'm sorry about the dogs, I owe them a bone. Word says pride cometh before a fall. It was just a matter of time before I slipped. Allison Alldaway might as well been a banana peel on a freshly waxed floor.

Anyway, after the accident I spent my money and fought like hell to keep my black ass from going to jail. I got the best white lawyer, the most liberal white judge and a non white jury. My mama, my pastor and my high school football coach were my character witnesses. My Mama cried; they always do. After a meeting with the Jacksonville Triad, the mayor, the state attorney, the Pro-ball team owner I plea dealed a reckless driving conviction. I was crucified in the media and by every black woman in northeast Florida for reckless eyeballing a white woman. I was kicked off the force six months ago and should have left town. But this is my town, my nightlife, my street life, my action, my life! This was J's Ville and I wasn't leaving.

Like so many women in my life, I believe I could get this town back. Even if she didn't want me right now. One day, she would need me and I'll be here for her. Until then I can make it out here on my own. I stacked paper and I knew people. Sure, I had the usual expenses, my kids, chromed out cars and the latest fashion, with my wrist and neck all iced out. I did all the things that players do. But I understood the art of parlaying money and financing the streets. Vice taught me that money rules everything around me, a hot dog vendor on the corner, a bank robber doing a stick up or a hooker giving a blow job, it's all about the paper, ain't nothing personal.

I got money backing an auto detail shop on the south side and a construction drywall company downtown. I got money in an exotic car company on the beach and a barbeque and fish joint on the north side. I'm in deep, too deep to leave.

Today, it's something new. I'm meeting my best friend Kareem, known on the street as Slick-Wit-It, aka, Slick. He wants to meet at Nubbie's restaurant, says some guys contacted him about a real estate deal. They need financing to buy the old shut down ocean way lumber mill and build a housing community on the property. Slick believes we can make millions, but he always believes we can make millions. What really counts is he is my best friend, which means, I'm in.

"Come lay down," Rosa moans.

Rosa or Rosemary Cruz has become my refuge through this ordeal. My confidant and lover, she moved me into her place on river road to hide away from many of my persecutors. With her, I may not be completely innocent but I'll never be guilty. Rosa, herself well-connected in city social circles as president of the Springfield Community Preservation Society, she also owns a club lounge and art gallery at Ninth and Main. We met at one of the mayor's charity golf and tennis galas, Rosa and I sipped Caribbean rum; she gave me the numbers to her crib, cell and job. I've been putting in work with her ever since. Sometimes sassy, sometimes classy but at forty-one our eleven year age difference seems to allow a level of comfort and ease I haven't found with women my own age.

She loves me and allows me in my own way to love her back and besides that, she's hot. From her thick puckered lips, dark eyes and road tar colored hair that hangs down past the shoulders of her sleek athletic body, her skin a shade lighter than maple syrup, Rosa is a beautiful woman whose body is a wonderland of pleasure for the man she allows within the sanctity of her arms and legs, she never has to beg for it.

I turn and slowly walk to the bed fitted with maroon satin sheets. Rosa's nude body under the sheets form curls and swells and brakes as beautiful as any Hawaiian surf.

She pulls the covers off and her skin still glistens with the oil of passion from love making the night before. She gives me a big smile and asks, "How about a game of two hand touch before you go?" I stare and smile. The chemistry between us has been crazy from the get-go. Not because I park my car at her place and my dick in her space, but that she's a real Puerto

Rican pussy cat and I'm cat nip. She's got a hook in my heart like it was a ten pound bass.

I stand over the bed and scan her naked body as if it were buried treasure just found, big black nipples on top of soft round titties, I start to get an erection, here "kitty kitty." I glance at the clock and its 6:30 am, still plenty of time before meeting Slick at Nubbie's.

"J. lay down," Rosa purred.

"Open up sassy, daddy's about to get nasty."

Then I fell into her longing as a sinner into a baptismal pool, bathing in the warmth of passion and appreciation that older women reciprocate.

Umm, the pussy's wet, but good and tight. I'll take my time and hit it right, slowly kissing and sucking on lips and tips. Making love like living po, head to toe. Take a deep breath then go down for mo.

Flip it, back it up, work it around, saddled up on her going to town!

I know Rosa's never done missionary work but she knew the position with her knees up, feet shoulders width apart, shoulder blades pressing down, booty thrusting up.

Lip to lip, hip to hip, I'm rolling thick and long this ain't no test ride I'm driving her home."Yes don't stop! Yes don't stop!" Rosa screams.

I kept my dick on the gas, my hands on her ass, shifting my stick in her three inch slit, we stopped at here spot when the clit got hot. She got off ahead of me but called out, come my love, come my love. I'm coming Rosa, I'm coming!

CHAPTER 3 – J'S VILLE

"**J**! YOU WANT some coffee? I just made a pot."

I woke to Rosa's sultry voice rolling through the room like smoke in an after-hours club, she had worked that pussy on me like it was a sleeping potion. I open my eyes to find myself lying nude, stretched across the bed like a starfish. Rosa had walked in from the kitchen and was picking up her panties, skirt and blouse from the bedroom floor, wearing nothing but a Puerto Rican flag necklace.

"I want you to come back to bed for a minute," I told her. "Minutes always turn into hours with you. You know that," she responded.

I turned my head towards the clock on the night stand. My eyes flickered as I focused on the time which was 8:15am. "I'm actually kind of proud of that," I told Rosa. "Anyway I've got to meet Slick at Nubbie's Restaurant at 9:00am."

"I worry when you're with Slick. Why don't you stay in and let momma take care of you today."

"Slick is my best friend and I'm his best manz. I got his back."

"God forbid you would break the code," says Rosa, "Come on I'll start your shower." "Not too hot," I responded as I followed her to the bathroom.

I was stepping out of the shower when local breaking news interrupted the Tom Joyner Morning Radio Show, they announced that homicide detectives were investigating a death in the San Marco area near River Road. I moved a little quicker and dressed a little faster; old habits die hard.

It was 8:45am when I walked out the door to a beautiful Jacksonville morning, stepping out in black Pele-Pele jean jacket and pants with ankle high black timberland boots. A black wife beater barely covering my chest and a pair of Dolce and Gabbana Fly Boy shades reflecting some of the shine I was letting off. Bad, Black and Bold, I was sharp as a Detroit pimp's switch blade and smelling fresher than a Ralph Lauren douche. At thirty years old I still have the lean muscular 190 pounds, six foot frame I had as a defensive back at the University of Central Florida. But after two knee surgeries, shoulder surgery and an hour or so of love making in the missionary position my stride is slow and easy this morning as I strolled like Secretariat to the starting gate, all bets on me.

The sky was extremely blue and the air was crisp as I move down the sidewalk to my Toyota Tundra pick-up truck, black with black tinted windows sitting on twenty two inch tires and BBS chrome rims. I reached the truck just twenty feet from the river bank then stopped to look out over the rippling Saint Johns River. A small fishing boat dropping crab traps passes to the sound of a honking seagull and water splashing against the concrete storm wall.

I step in and crank the truck then drive to the corner of River Road and San Marco Blvd where two drunk white guys fight in the parking lot next to a convenience store. A block further, a black male darts out from the side street being chased by a Jacksonville Sheriff Officer who's holding a shotgun close to his chest, six young black males sit handcuffed on the curve with police guns drawn and a helicopter circling overhead. I pass then hear a shotgun blast. I slowed down but did not stop.

I had driven only three short blocks when I saw the flashing lights, the yellow tape, the evidence van and Vice.

My pulse rate quickened, eyes squinted and I slowly exhaled. I had to pull over and check it out. I no longer had a badge but I still had the juice, the kind of juice that flows through any real vice cop when it's time to go get the bad guys, you might say, wolves run with wolves.

As I came up on the scene I spotted a familiar face, Kenny Keyes. Kenny was a local street cop who was well known for keeping lots of side action. Kenny got me to invest in a 'can't miss' racing dog he bought. Well, the dog never won and I lost four thousand dollars, he owes me some favors.

I pull my truck off the street onto the grassy lawn of the red brick house with the over sized porch and lower the driver's window to get Kenny's attention. He left his position on the sidewalk and came to my driver's side door. He greeted me with a big smile. "J! Good to see you, man! Where've you been? You stay over this way?"

Not wanting to be specific, I told him I was just lying low for now. "So, what happened here?"

"Well, the victim is a gang member named, Cornelius Walker, a.k.a. Corndog. He's said to have been a lieutenant in a gang of hoodlums called the Voodoo Zombie's."

"Is that a new gang?" I asked.

"They haven't been around long but they got a lot of people scared, although no one's going to fear this guy again."

"He's dead?" I asked Kenny.

"Corndog's been cooked and served. Somebody opened up a can of whip ass on him for real; he's got bones broke, blunt force trauma and he's been sliced up like a trillion cut diamond. He must have put up a fight though. There's busted furniture and fixtures all through the house. Not to mention all the blood everywhere. This is the third case like this in the last ten days."

Word says the wicked will be ruled guilty and condemned to death. "Are there any witnesses?" I asked.

"A few people reported seeing an athletically built male in dark clothes about 6:00am." I quickly thought of the dark figure I saw from the window earlier.

"This is your type of case," Kenny said to me.

"Who's working it?" I asked.

"Detective Bennie 'Big Biscuit' Bradley and Detective Joe 'Jelly Belly' Jackson got the case."

"Biscuit and Jelly, you have got to be kidding me Kenny. The only way those two plus size brothers will solve this case is if the perpetrators left a trail of bacon and eggs."

"We sure miss you out here, J."

"Thanks, Kenny. I've got to meet a friend. We'll talk soon." I let the window up then slowly drove away thinking about the case. I can't help it. It's in my blood. Who would know something? Who was the man in the silhouette on the river bank? The twenty minute drive to Nubbie's gave me plenty of time to think; to think of my time on the force, how much J'Ville need's me and how much I missed them too.

Off interstate 95 North and a slow ride up Martin Luther King Boulevard, I turned on Soutel Drive and rode along the frontlines of black urban America. Lines to the cemetery start forming early literally and figuratively. A funeral procession ahead has traffic moving at a pace that allows me the opportunity to suck in the surroundings like a big ol' blunt. You'd have to be real high not to feel this environment deep inside.

Unhealthy and malnourished nomads roam the streets as homeless shelters and crack houses release their patrons to go out and hustle a days pay. Cars with candy coated paint jobs sit on top of 26 inch rims, hanging like Christmas tree ornaments in street corner traps, driven by brothers who haven't had a valid driver's license sense child support court took them. They're planning their next hostel corporate take-over or convenience store stick up.

I was passing bus stops where girls too young and women too old stand pregnant looking to drop a baby then get a check, oh you know what they say, first and the fifteenth is ghetto holiday. School aged children walking the sidewalks on a school day still wearing their pajamas while eating a bag of potato chips for breakfast, forget home schooling this is hood schooling.

White businessmen, doctors, lawyers and preachers drive through the communities where the night before some young black trick might have got them sick, their wives woke up itching and burning. Daily chatter is interrupted by screams of, "they killed my son or they killed my brother". Communities have been deserted by the middle aged and middle class. They got government jobs and government housing and got the hell out. The young, the old and the poor were left to fend for themselves.

Like so many black areas of town just off so many Martin Luther King Boulevards, it's become a black refugee camp with young jiggaz in groups of three, five and seven next to tents and signs. Car wash five dollars, jeans and shirts twenty dollars. Bootleg sneakers and CD's. How much? "How much you want to pay?" Like anywhere else, commerce rules. You need used tires for your car, it's here. You need a used gun with the serial number filed off, it's here. They're out here on their on just trying to be grown, they're only role model left home chasing a bitch and some patron. They wanted to grow up and be the first black president until they saw them KKracKers trying to kill him, now what?

It's not that people on this side of town don't know that the sky's the limit. They're told every Sunday that prosperity is going to rain down on them. They use the healing oils and prayer cloths, it's just that every morning they go out hoping that prosperity has fallen and all they find is two tears in a bucket and a dead body in the dumpster.

CHAPTER 4 – NUBBIE'S

NUBBIE'S RESTAURANT AND lounge is a little soul food breakfast and supper joint on Soutel Drive in the Northwest quadrant of Jacksonville. An area known for robberies, assaults, car jackings, killings and retaliation killings, and oh yeah, spirited black churches, Raines High School and Jenkins Barbeque.

Jacksonville police department has listed it as zone thirteen. If you live there you're more likely than not an unlucky son of a bitch. But zone thirteen was my territory, J'sville. Till pussy got me fucked and I lost my title and my status.

With its nightclubs and back alleys, zone thirteen is where the action is and Nubbie's sits right in the heart of it all, Located in the old XYZ Liquor store building. A restaurant in the front of the building with a little liquor lounge in the back.

The spot where there was always music, drinking, gambling, tricking and every now and then some killing.

I turned into Nubbie's parking lot. Before getting out of the truck I opened the arm rest and took out the ankle holster with my favorite little 25 caliber pearl handle pistol. I'm deadly accurate with it. You can shake me but don't get me stirred up. Just because I lost my badge doesn't mean I lost my license to kill. I strapped it around my right ankle then got out of the truck walking to the restaurant door. It's time to meet Slick and do the damn thing.

As I cross the parking lot a young black man standing at the right corner of the building quickly approaches me, hat to the side, mouth full of gold, pants criss-crossed hanging down to the ground. He's holding a red brick in one hand and a kitchen butcher knife in the other. "Give me the keys to your truck and your north side taxes, unless you want to strip and I take the pants and the pockets with it", he said.

I be damn if this bitch ain't trying to jack me! I pulled up my right pant leg revealing the twenty-five caliber then pulled out a twenty dollar bill. I don't usually throw pearl to the swine but I told him I was going to give him a dove and let him live, any other day I'd air him out but I got other business this morning. He took it from my hand and ran off. When are black men going to stop losing their lives over this bullshit, stay in school.

Just as I reached the door it opened. A young woman stepped one foot out while still yelling back inside. "You tell him I'm looking for him and I'm gonna get my child support," she said. "I don't care who da baby look like." It was Nephertitti Green, the baby making machine. Well known around these parts.

Nephertitti made her living by collecting child support. One shot of that tail will get you a court ordered paternity test in the mail.

They say she can take a man's saliva and make a baby. She just dropped her ninth child but she still got a body like Beyonce and butty like two beach volley balls. Wearing red high top converse basketball shoes, tennis ball yellow biker shorts and a purple t-shirt with the words pro life across the front, she turns her attention to me. Looking me up and down. "So, what's up playboy?" she asks. "My doctor says I can start dating in a couple of weeks."

"I'm tied up," I tell her, "but you might check the internet for match-a-freak." She then holds the palm of her left hand up to my face and says, "Whatever," as she steps out the door and walks toward the street. I thought to myself the crack babies of the 80's have come of age and the community that neglected them is reaping a bitter harvest.

I stood watching Nephertitti walk away until a voice yelled from inside the restaurant. "Come inside here and close the door, stop letting in flies."

Nubbie had a big voice like an old Baptist preacher. It thundered high above the chatter of the patrons, the juke box and the sizzling fry pan coming from the kitchen.

"Alright brother," I replied. I never argue with a person who's food I'm about to eat. Nubbie, whose real name is Levander Williams, Jr. has no hands or feet. Rumor has it he used to pedal moonshine, meth and stolen cars for some ruthless rednecks. Then when they caught him stashing product for himself the H.K.I.C. (Head KKracKer In Charge) had his hands and feet tide to the railroad tracks. He's sitting in one of those new electric wheel chairs down at the right end of the counter using those two prong steel artificial hands to hold a cigarette and read the sports page.

Across the counter from Nubbie is Earl, a sixty something year old dude who still dresses from the seventies. With his big colorful hats, big collar shirts and bell bottom pants over platform shoes. I throw him a black power sign and he yells, right on brother.

In a booth to my right with the table covered in horse racing forms is Atlanta, better known as AT. He can give you the breakers, the closers, the turf conditions and the lucky numbers for the day. "I got a cold lock in the third race at Calder race track, he says; the three horse, with a three letter name and he's thirty to one, come hala at your boy." I pull the black lizard skin money clip from my pocket and peel off ten Benjamins. "Give me three hundred to win, place, show and keep the hundred for your tip," I tell him. That quick he had taken it from my hand.

Pacing the floor talking to everybody and nobody is Can't-Chance-It. The former college professor of theology and astrology whom professionals say had a mental break down. Ever since then he's been drawing a crazy check and hanging around Nubbie's prognosticating. I see everyone but Slick.

"Ain't seen you for a minute, where you been Pretty Brown?" asked Nubbie.

"I've been operating off radar but I'm still here."

"Well, you watch your back out there. I heard what went down with the grey girl" (referring to the white women, Allison Alldaway).

"Well, every day these Pharisees trying to crucify Obama, why should it be any different in my life," I responded.

The Kitchen door swings open and Nubbie's seventy four year old mother comes walking through with a hand full of clean saucers. "Good morning Mom." Her name's Ms. Annie Lee, but everyone here calls her

Mom. "Good morning, baby," she says with a big smile, wearing a white and pink horizontal stripped uniform dress. "What can I get you?"

"I'll have a cup of coffee for now mom. I'm waiting on somebody."

"Your man been here and left," Nubbie yells from the end of the counter. "What?" I ask him, as I look at my watch to see it was almost 10 o'clock. "Yeah, he said you'll probably be late for his funeral too."

"Mom let me get that coffee to go please."

"Why don't you call him?" asked Earl. "Cause he never has a cell phone that works, but I'm planning to get him a new one when we finish this business today," I explained.

"So, what do you know about the Night Stalker?" Can't-Chance-It asked me in a low whispery voice as he passed my stool. "What do you mean?" I asked him. "Somebody's got the brothers scared, real scared. They don't want to be caught without their finger on the trigger. Someone is using Cheney's enhanced interrogation techniques to murder every drug dealer, pimp and hustler in J'ville. I heard he sliced and diced a boy up over in San Marco last night. Police have no suspects at this time and time is running out. Many parish in the pits because they have no regard for he that is lost, remember your deliverance is at hand don't leave without it, evil deeds comes in threes, be bold and mighty forces will deliver you."

I responded to Can't-Chance-It as if that shit he said made sense. "Well, damn! I said, maybe you should come with me and watch my back in case these dudes haven't been up front with us and something goes wrong."

He paused as if to think over my suggestion then answered, "You won't go alone, but I can't chance it."

CHAPTER 5 – THE 411

AS I WALKED out of Nubbie's Restaurant sipping on my coffee my steps seem quick. Hearing Cant-chance-it made me anxious. I paused for a quick gut check inside my truck. With the key in the ignition my spirit said wait as my fight or flight senses were clicking on again and I didn't know why. I thought back to the early morning, to that feeling that woke me; the dark figure on the river bank, the murdered gang member. Something about this shit ain't right.

It was then as I stared out the windshield across the almost one acre parking lot. It caught my eye. Behind the building that sat at the far side of the lot. It was facing the street, eight to ten inches tall, grayish, blackish, brownish. Did someone lose it, did somebody drop it off or did it wonder off and get lost? A puppy, a little puppy sitting with his head and eyes focused out across the four lane street.

I watched as it walked five or six yards toward the street and stop. It sat and looked at each car pass as if it were counting the intervals between each one. It moved closer to the street. I cranked my truck and moved closer to what looked like the puppy's projected launching spot from the curve to the roadway. Had it been in another area of town crossing the four lane roadway, it might not have held such peril.

The Southside, the beaches, even downtown, some white person would stop their car in the middle of traffic, get out and stop all four lanes until the puppy crosses. This ain't that. On the Northside, a brother doesn't yank his whip unless it's a honey walking down the side walk, so fine he gots to hala. For sure a sister is not going to stop her car in the street to pick up a stray dog. There was something about his plight that spoke to me. Being lost and wondering, trying to get back to the life you know. Trying to get back to what you know best. Sometimes you just need a hand, a hand to carry you for a minute, to protect you, someone to see you through the valley of the shadow of death. Who else better to be your friend than the one who knows you need a friend.

I don't know if it was timing or a leap of faith, but while I sat looking for the deeper meaning, he must have seen his opportunity. The little funny colored short haired dog with big black eyes and floppy ears lunged from the curve into the roadway. With quick prancing steps as if it was trying to adjust to the texture of the pavement, it crossed the first lane, then second and into the center lane. There he stopped and sat. I grabbed the door handle with my left hand. I opened the door and jumped from the truck all at the same time. I raced to cross the street ahead of the next car. Its head turned toward me and it looked so at ease. It seemed so sure that this treacherous journey would end well. The little puppy seemed to know he would be saved; that he had a higher calling than to die in this street.

The old folks around where I grew up call this standing in the gap for someone. The gap is the doorway between good and evil, life and death. It's how you come out of any ghetto to have a successful life. You have to be let out. The good and the bad around you have to decide that you are worth saving. The good pray for you and the bad make you get out of the car before they go to rob the corner store. The good hope every game for you not to get hurt then praise your accomplishments. The bad give you a pass to walk home after practice and not get shot. That's the reason you never come up out of the ghetto and tell folks you did it, you made it and you don't owe nobody. You have to always remember, somebody stood in the gap for you. Somebody was your hero that plucked you from the pavement and placed you in your paradise.

In that thought, I had scooped the little puppy with my left hand and turned extending my right hand to traffic. The cars slowed and with a few strides then a lunge, I was on the sidewalk with my new friend. With both hands, I held it up to meet face to face. Black button eyes and a flat wrinkled pushed in face. He also had this brown spot right in the middle of his chest. I looked him over and he checked me out. What next? He had no tag nor collar. Who'd he belong to? How did he get here?

Would he stand any chance if I left him here? No! The next time I see him he might be loaded down with fleas and ticks or even recruited to fight for Michael Vick. It's moments like these that my favorite Bible verse taught to me as a boy in Sunday school comes into my head. Psalms 41:1; Blessed are those who have shown mercy to the weak, the Lord delivers that person in times of trouble. "Well, little friend, it seems you're the weak and I've come to your rescue. So, the Lord is supposed to deliver me in my time of trouble. What trouble could there be on a day like today," I said to the puppy almost expecting some reply. "Now, let's go." I walked over to the truck and opened the door then reached across the console and placed him on the front passenger seat and hopped in.

I paused to look it over just one more time and wondered what it might be thinking. Maybe it's thinking, I'm the one being rescued. That I'm the weak and it and the Lord are going to deliver me, 41:1?

So Lord, I've had regard for the weak, now you owe me one, because in this world I live everybody's got a gun. I crank the truck then pull out of the parking lot. And Lord one more thing, watch over Slick, don't let this be no trick.

CHAPTER 6 – SORRY I'M LATE

AS I TURNED onto North Main Street towards the lumber yard, my little wrinkly faced puppy's eyes focused on my every move. Driving past the barber shops, pawn shops and chicken joints of the black community, I wondered where did all these Chinese restaurants come from and why am I buying my hair products from a Korean.

The bail bondsman, check cashing shops, rent to own furniture businesses and buy-here pay-here car lots. Throw in some weed, coke, rap music, senseless violence and there you have it: life in the black community. Love it or leave it.

As I continued up Main Street and crossed over the old trout river bridge, I knew I was venturing into new territory. I was leaving the in your face lifestyle of urban black America for the behind closed doors of old Klan's country. I was now in Ocean Way. Four lanes became two. Crowded concrete became long patches of woods and trees with wooden mailboxes next to dirt roads that snake deep into your curiosity.

The smell of fried food and road work gave way to the sulfur smell of smoke from the brewery and lumber yards. Klan camps have now given way to fish camps and camp grounds. Moose lodges and Knights of Columbus halls are where boy and girl scouts meet. Strip malls with boutiques, convenience shops and of course, a Chinese restaurant. I think if someone builds a strip mall on Mars, a Chinese person will have a restaurant in it and two doors down will be a Vietnamese nail shop.

But the main industry here seems to be churches. Baptist churches,

Pentecostal churches, Holiness churches and more Baptist churches. The only thing more numerous than churches is pick up trucks.

In the distance, I could see the smoke stacks from the old lumber mill. I knew it wasn't far from my turn. The old mill has been closed now for some time as most of the paper mill jobs have moved up north and west. Good ole boy southern ignorance for innovation kept the plants from advancing with the times. The Northern Mills now owned by Asian and European investors have gobbled up territory until they literally sucked all the life out of the stand alone operations like this one. All that's left now is for the local city government to approve the money for demolition of the vacant facilities; then clear the land for sale to home developers. According to Slick, the guys we're meeting needed money to get in on the action.

Until then, the abandoned saw houses with their yards and yards of conveyer belts that carried logs to the saw blades sit quiet. The buildings where thousands of pounds of bark and wood product were burned and the chimneys that would pour out a sulfuric odor filled smoke that engulfed all of Northeast Florida are empty.

All sit as deserted as a Wild West ghost town, but they're no ghost of darkness to fear here, only the dark hearted jigga with a gun or a knife that will make you a ghost.

There were deep pits dug on the vast acreage to dispose of unprocessed residue. The pits, which are now partially filled with water, serve as death traps for stray dogs or rodents who venture too deep over the edge. The dirt from the pit stands along side the massive holes like fields of Egyptian pyramids.

As a teenager, I would sometimes come here with my Uncle Tan. He was an old woodsman who made his living in the old trade known as pulp wooding. Men in this line of work would go out each day and secure patches of unclaimed pine tree rich land in there log trucks. In the middle of undeveloped forest they would cut prime trees all day. Toppling forty and fifty foot trees then cutting them into eight to ten foot logs. After a long day and a truck full of three hundred pound logs the 'Pulpwooder' drives his bounty to the mill. As a thirteen year old boy I would anticipate that end of day trip to the mill. He'd always have me get out of the truck at the front gate then drive on to have his load plucked from the truck and weighed. Uncle Tan would always say it was too dangerous for a young boy around all that machinery.

So, the mill was always a place of danger in my mind. Even to this day and this very moment, as I approach, my back bows as a cat stalking. Is it that memory or the reality that I'm headed to this secluded spot for a money deal with people I don't know and have never met. Since the mill closed, there have been numerous accounts of rapes and murders. The type of guys you meet at a place like this are not the type that can go to the local bank or credit union to apply for a loan. In these deals, I'm my own bank manager, teller and collection agency. Board meetings in these streets are going to consist of hustlers, pimps, prostitutes and pushers. But every business needs flow and since I'm not a cop right now I'm a pusher. I push dough.

A hundred yards from my turn, a car is pulling out. It makes a left turn and is coming towards me. I slow down to observe closer. The car creeps toward me never picking up speed. It's a late model convertible, '65 or '66 Chevy with white interior, the top's down, big chrome mag rims and three occupants. The three are looking at me as intense as I am focusing on them. I don't let down the tinted window so they can't see me clearly. But I can see them. The driver was black, real black. He was African, a real African, like the ones you see in those save the children commercials with a round face, pointed features with yellow eyes and teeth. The front passenger was white, not a white man, but whiter, Albino. He had ghostly gray eyes and hair like white sheep's wool. The rear passenger sitting in the middle of the back seat was a dark skinned brother with multiple gold teeth and chin hair. He had shoulder length black dreads and a long jagged scar running down the left side of his face. All three looked to be in their mid-twenties. I know stick up kids and body snatchers when I see them. If they're not either then they're phone book delivery men, but the new issue ain't out! We pass. I make my turn and stop to see if they turn around, if they think my guard is down, from early in the night my senses been telling me something ain't right get ready to fight. They continue driving then so do I. What you got us into Slick? Young jackers, a deserted location- this smells like smoke, the type of smoke that leads to fire; gunfire.

I should not have been late. I should not have let Slick come alone. When there's money on the line that means lives are on the line. These are huge gambles and there some wagers you can't afford to lose. Slick would lie for me, die for me and put his left hand on the Bible and hold his right hand high and testify for me. Why am I not on time for him? I slowly snaked along the white sandy dirt road barely wide enough for two vehicles side by side. The road with a three foot ditch on each side carved through a forest of pine and oak trees with thick shrubbery and palmetto saw palms. The locals now litter these woods with garbage and old washers, dryers and sofas. I glance at the little puppy. "You know it's your fault we're late, don't say anything when we see Slick. I'll do all the talking, as if you could actually say something to get me through this."

I continue to talk to the little button eyed puppy until I reach an old aluminum gate. The gate blocks the entrance to the old mill property. There's a big "No Trespassing" sign hanging on it and it looks like it had recently been pulled close. I bring the truck to a stop and look around before I unlock the door and open it. "Be right back," I say to the puppy as I step out. Walking to the gate a light rain begins to fall. In the middle of a beautiful sunny day a dark cloud has smothered this property. I push the gate open as the rain comes down a little heavier then run back to the truck and cut on the windshield wipers as I jump in. I roll in past the gate and onto the property with its boarded up windows and doors, a town that now gets an occasional visit from graffiti artist, or a bum passing through looking for a roof to sleep under or some thug boys looking for a spot to drop a body.

No sign of Slick's Chevy Tahoe truck and not one note from his booming sound system that's always playing whether it's parked or moving. There's no sign of the sun now and the only sounds I hear around the place is a few black birds crowing. I stop and survey the area as the windshield wipers slash back and forth thinking maybe Slick didn't show, maybe nobody showed. I think of leaving but is that fear? Because I've been out of action for a while, out of the line of fire for a while. This place is a backdrop for trouble. I was a little jumpy, but for Slick I've got to see this through. A gravel service road to my left partially covered with grass and tree limbs called to me through the rain. The service road ran around the main property to the pit fields. Kind of like your throat running down into your stomach, stuff in there ain't pretty. I begin to follow the little crooked road past the haunting buildings that no doubt have been witness to terrible things since the mill's closing. I peer through the windshield at every bump, tree limb, pot hole and blade of grass. They all seem to speak at me and say, "Go back." The little puppy seemed anxious and started to tremble. Jacksonville is well deserving of the nickname Killville, where jiggaz kill for the hobby and have no remorse. Out here you can't click you heels together three times and go home when you find yourself in the shit. This is J'sville, she is my Rome and I am her Gladiator.

I opened up the arm rest of the truck's center console then reached in and grab a couple of extra clips for the 25 caliber and slid them in my left front pocket. I carry extra clips like most people carry extra credit cards. Rows of dirt pyramids sit undisturbed with weeds and brush three feet high growing on some sections. Pyramid's next to thirty and forty foot deep pits. There's an odor of deep earth and decaying animal carcasses. I drove down the rows of pyramids and past water filled pits. The deeper in I drove the worse it smells.

There! There it is! The silver four door Chevy Tahoe with tinted windows and 24 inch chrome rims. It's parked at the end of a row of those huge dirt mounds. Slicks truck, but where's Slick? I stop my truck about ten paces behind his. What's most obvious is the rear windows are busted out. I'm so anxious to see Slick, I forget all my years of police training. I don't grab the sawed-off shotgun in the utility compartment under the rear passenger seat. I didn't take the nine millimeter strapped under the dash board.

The rain had eased to a light drizzle as I walked slowly to the vehicle and along the driver's side. Most of the windows had been shot out. There must have been at least fifteen large caliber bullet holes along the side of the truck and the driver side window was busted completely out. There was blood splattered all over the front dash board and windshield. The dark grey leathered driver's seat was smeared with thick maroon colored blood. Someone had bled deep. Slick is nowhere inside the vehicle. On the ground there's a trail of bloody muddy water leading around one of the dirt pyramids. I follow the trail while softly calling his name, "Slick… Slick…Slick." On the opposite side of the dirt pyramid the trail leads over the edge of a large pit. SLICK! I yell his name as if I were Jesus calling Lazarus from the grave.

I get to the edge and look down and there he is. As if someone tried to roll him into the pit half filled with water but he stuck to the side.

Face up wearing a number thirty two Jacksonville Jaguar's Football jersey, baggy jeans that have been dragged down to his knees and a pair of teal and black Jordan's. All smeared with blood. I kneel and step the four feet inside the cone shaped pit to Slick's motionless body. I move close to him and continue to call his name, "Slick, talk to me, Slick". On his right side I reach across his chest to his left shoulder and put my left hand under his right shoulder and lift his torso. I knelt in the dirt with his torso in my lap and his head against my chest. "Slick, I got you, I got you, baby. Stay with me Slick. We got too much to do. You and I got great battles to fight. We got great adventures ahead and territory to conquer. Hold on for me, Slick. We can still win. I promise you this is just the first quarter. We got a full game to play."

It was then I heard a faint cough. Bruised, bullet riddled and blooded. His eyes opened and connected with mine. His tongue pushed blood from his mouth. "You missed the kickoff," he said. "I'm sorry I was late," I said as my eyes began to water. He cracked a smile and with what turned out to be his last breath he said, "Don't be late for my funeral." His body went limp; his eyes went dark and black. A single stream of blood flowed from the side of his mouth. Slick! Slick! I called to him with tears flowing from my eyes and snot running from my nose. "I'm sorry I was late, please forgive me. Please come back. God don't do this, please. How could you give me a best friend, and then take him back. Jesus, Jesus, help me, Jesus. Please, Jesus step down from your throne and help me, Jesus." Slick was gone.

Then like a crack of lightening from a distance, I heard the sound of a pistol cocking. The puppy barking, then a gunshot rang out. "I'll see you again," I said to Slick as I lay the empty vessel that once held his soul to the ground. Jesus please deliver me from the hand of he who slay my friend. Then with one long stride, I lunged from the pit like a black panther from tall grass. Crouched for ultimate fighting, I reach and pull the 25 caliber from my ankle holster with my right hand and took an extra clip from my left pocket. Safety clicked off. Murder mode clicked on. I started my sprint around the dirt pyramid not waiting to reach or see my target. With every stride, I was busting off a clip as fast as they would rip. Both arms extended straight in front of me, my right hand popping off twenty five's. My left hand was holding an extra clip in a fist except for my middle finger, which was straight up. My middle finger I want to show this perpetrator as I read him his right to go straight to hell. No need to know who this person is first, no need to know what their motive was or if they were provoked or felt threatened. This Herod had killed my John the Baptist and I was coming like the Christ to send him to eternal damnation.

They'll know it's on when my bullets hit the bone.

As I rounded the dirt pile with the twenty-five jumping in my hand like a baby jack rabbit I found my self in an O.K. corral draw down at point blank range with the Albino and the African. Both positioned near the rear of Slicks SUV. They unleashed a bee swarm of black lead as I quickly dove for cover in front of the truck's hood. You don't hear lead till it's already passed your head so I'm still alive. I never stopped firing. They were getting off rounds, from what appeared to be a 9mm and a pump shot gun, back pedaling as they fired.

These bastards trying to cut off my life line but I ain't heard Jesus say it's my time. BOOM! BOOM! BOOM! I keep busting back, fight'n off what a brother fears most, another Black.

I remember what Can't-Chance-It told me, "Be bold and mighty forces will deliver me." I looked up over the hood as I continued to fire and yell, "You're going to die, mother fucker, and I'm going to kill you." Out of my view they had stopped firing. I turned to look down the passenger side of the truck and I'm face to face with the Albino and the pump shotgun. He pumped then fired as I lunged back behind cover. The pellets shredded the metal from the side of the truck as they skirted past me. The Albino wants my shirt wet but I ain't hit yet. He continued to spit till he unloaded the bitch. With my back to the hood, I spun from left side to right side. Firing till my trigger finger cramped. When one clip emptied I'd jam in another.

They had stopped firing but I never let up. Not until I heard car doors close and an engine rev. I ran out from behind Slick's truck to see the convertible kicking up dirt as it raced around the service road. The African was driving; the Albino in the front seat and the Black Dread was in the middle rear.

I gave a short chase still firing shots, determined not to let them get away. I run back to my truck. Thinking I could catch them but discovering they had let the air out of my tires. I glanced inside, and then opened the driver's door. With my cup of rage and sorrow already full. It now over flowed as I found the puppy had been killed. Was it that first gunshot or all the rest? The button eyed, wrinkled face puppy was dead. He sounded the warning that saved my life. With his life he delivered me from trouble.

Then with one burst, I began to sprint down the service road fueled with a deadly mix of pain and revenge. Firing my weapon at the image I had of the Albino, the African and the Black Dread.

Once the pistol was empty, I cried out, "Till your last breath! I will hunt you. Till I see you take your last breath! You killed my dog! You killed my dog! You killed my dog and my puppy too!"

CHAPTER 7 – MY MANZ

SLICK! WHAT HAPPENED here? Why did this happen here? Had I known this was a battlefield and not a board room or known you were meeting urban snipers and not sales associates, I would not have let this battle start without me leading the charge.

I buried the little puppy in the sand after thanking it for standing in the gap for me then pulled my friend from the dirt. I wiped the blood from his face and brushed the sand from his hair then lifted and cradled him in my arms and walked him from the pit. I had let him come to this place alone but I would not leave him. From the Mill I walked the sandy road through the woods to the highway carrying my friend in my arms.

I walked the two lane highway towards Jacksonville. Barely aware of the rubberneckers or good Samaritans offering assistance, we had come from so many street wars together. Now would not be any different. The friend only God could have sent me.

Remembering how as nine and ten year olds we'd venture through the area woods, we would scout for birds, rabbits and squirrels. He'd drive the bicycle and I would ride on the handle bars. We played little league football together. When we were older he took me on my first motorcycle ride and we started a band together as teenagers. We chased girls and smoked our first joint together. Slick grew up across the street from me. He was the fifth youngest in a family of eight. Both parents were in the home; which is not typical of many black households. Statistics say seventy percent of black children are raised by a single parent.

But Slick's two parent household was no fairytale. His daddy, Mr. Roscoe Jones, owned a landscaping company and worked hard laying sod and mowing lawns. It was hard work especially for a man born practically handicapped with limited use of one leg. He was still a good businessman. Too bad he was not a good father. Like many black men he was never taught how to love his wife and raise his children. His wife, Mrs. Laretha, paid for it. Every Friday and Saturday night he'd get drunk and race up and down the neighborhood streets in his Chevy. Stopping periodically in his front yard, he would get out of his car and go inside the house and punch Mrs. Laretha a couple of times and drag her by her hair to the car. The whole time calling her a jigger bitch. Then racing up and down the street with her screaming and crying in the passenger seat. Through it all, Slick seemed wild and happy. His daddy gave him the nickname "Slick" because he was always stealing and drinking his beer. He'd drink some and sell the rest to the bums on the corner. Slick had game before Kobe or Diddy.

During high school, he ran numbers for the Cuba and Bolito houses back before we got the lottery. He would sell over priced candy and snacks to kids in school. On weekends, at Smokey's Night limit, the lil' juke joint across the railroad tracks in the area known as 'The Bottom'. Slick would collect the houses cut from dice and card games going on in the back of the building. He'd take that money to Smokey and by the end of the night Smokey would break him off twenty five or thirty dollars. To the other teenage guys in the community he was so cool he seemed to have his own soundtrack as he moved from one hustle to the next. He was 'Slick-Wit-It'.

He did all that and still played football, basketball, and ran track. I'll never forget the day there was a baseball game and track meet going on at the same time. Slick tripled in the run in the first inning. Then he changed clothes and ran to the track to compete in the hundred yard dash. He ran a school record before going back to the baseball game and hitting a home run. What he could have become had he practiced or for that matter did home work. I played and worked hard at it, but Slick was a natural. I learned a lot about the hustle game from him also. But Slick would never let me in. When he made his runs he would tell me I couldn't go with him. He'd say I came from a good family and if something happened to me, they would forever blame him. He'd say "C.J. you can get so far out there that the world will not let you go back and you can't get out there just yet."

He should have gotten a scholarship to a big time school and done big things. But the beginning of our senior year of high school he got busted for pedaling home made sex tapes of him and teenage girls, thirty or forty different Hannah Montana's. Slick was jumping them school girls like a juiced up Jesuit.

Well, he got ninety days in juvie and probation. No scholarship, no big time ball playing. I went on to the University of Central Florida and a football scholarship. He came to every home game and I made sure there was always a ticket for him. Even though we talked and hung out as much as possible, our lives were headed in different directions. I was running touchdowns while he ran numbers. I studied criminology while he became a criminal. Not to make excuses but it was more or less his destiny. The hand he was dealt, then played. The streets and the hustle game became his whole life. I became a cop. I would tell him to find a good girl to chill with. That a quality established woman would really upgrade his life. He would tell me he was interviewing every night and when he finds her, I will be the best manz at his wedding. From that point on he was my manz and I was his best manz.

I didn't lose my friend to a suicide bomber in Bagdad or a mountain fighter in Afghanistan. My friend was lost to the war of ignorance, the war of self hatred, the war of chicken -shit, shoot you in the back, drive by bastards. This is the dark side of the dark race.

Human Rottweilers and Pit bulls, spawned in abandoned coochees, left to incubate in deprived social, cultural and intellectual squalor. They're nourished with hate, violence, drugs and self indulgence. They come like a thief in the night to steal and to kill. These home grown terrorist can only be stopped by abortion or a bullet. I will bring light to these giant cock roaches. The light that flashes from the barrel when the bullet blast.

Slick, this will not end with you being a victim in the crime section of the local paper. "V" will not stand for victim, but victory. The long hard road to redemption is lined with land mines, sniper fire and dead bodies, but if the Profits were right then magnificent kingdoms await us. I'll look for you there.

My then exhausted body collapsed in the arms of the emergency medical team that had been called by passing motorist, I then gathered the strength and recall to give my account to the police.

CHAPTER 8 – SOS

I SPENT THE NEXT few days laying low at Rosa's, licking the wounds of a lost battle and mourning the death of my friend. I ain't gonna slack till I get them bastards back. I've been making a list of every dope house, dogfight and crap game in town. The type places the Albino, African and Black Dread might hang out.

Was Slick's death a random killing or was it a set up? Are these guys responsible for the rise in murders around Jacksonville? So far the streets ain't talking. Either nobody knows or they're too scared to tell.

I'm gonna run down every snitch in this city till somebody talks. Between searching for clues and plotting my revenge, I sat on the corner of the bed staring at the floor hoping for forgiveness from Slick and telling him how sorry I am.

I may have said it a thousand times but a thousand is not enough for letting my friend suffer alone and die so brutally. I will never forgive my self and I will never stop chasing the evil that has brought this into our lives.

My soul cried the blues and tears flowed from my eyes. I turn to check the time on the nightstand clock; it's 9:30am. Slick's funeral is at 11:00am. Rest assured my friend this is only a comma at this point in your life, not the period.

After a quick shower I slipped into a black thin lapel boss black single breast suit with a black Ralph Lauren black label long sleeve shirt and black boot style Salvatore Farragamo shoes. I had about an hour before the funeral. That was time enough for me to make a quick stop along the way.

One of my best sources of street information was Sonja. Sonja O'Sullivan, at least that's the name I had here listed as when she was my best confidential informant. She's a 5'1" coke bottled shape, fifty two year old SBF (Single Black Female) who still looks like a jet magazine centerfold. She works part time as a cashier at Winn-Dixie grocery store, but full time she and her girlfriends work the gambling boat. They refer to themselves as the 'Trick Train'. The boat's patrons are mainly male gamblers. The girls would spend the evening looking for winners.

A man can be as rich as shit but he'll give it all up for that three inch slit.

Once they catch something on the boat and get back to shore. It's off to the motel, or apartment or maybe just a dark area of the parking lot. Thirty for a hand job, a hundred for straight sex and five hundred for an all night round the world. They will accept cash or betting chips. The men get quick easy sex that they have control over. NO begging before and no cuddling afterwards. Women, like Sonja, get paid. Everybody's happy. As they say on the street, an even swap ain't no swindle.

I met Sonja four years ago after she had written her phone number on a grocery receipt during one of my purchases. She was sweet and sexy and I dig older women. So, I looked her up. Right away, she wanted to borrow money from me and was very eager to have sex. I know the streets too well not to know something much deeper was at play. Instead I took her to dinner. Then the cigar bar for martini's and smokes. We talked and I learned that through a domino of circumstances she was a little down on her luck. So, she hustled to make up the slack. I never look to take advantage of the weak. I believe in playing with the real ballers not those on injured reserve. She also told me she was HIV positive. She said she picked it up from a city bus driver who traded free rides for sex. Unfortunately there are those who will take advantage of the weak. That's a shame. Thing was she knew people. She knew lots of people. She knew what was happening on the streets and where it was happening. Dudes have a tendency to run their mouth while they're fucking. Especially young dudes, young dudes Sonja preferred not to service. She said young jiggaz wanted to fuck for hours then not want to pay or tip.

I made it clear I would not risk having sex with her but I would put her on the department's payroll as a confidential informant. We chose the name Sonja O'Sullivan and it's all I've called her since. Sonja and I are still cool even though I'm off the force.

I left Rosa's and headed just west of downtown Jacksonville. Going to see Sonja was not without peril. She resides in a world of shady dealings. Where cut throats and throat cutters abound. She lives where lawlessness is law, where the news of the day is the daily arrest report and the mounting death toll. Where she lives, your life is summed up with three numbers; your birth certificate to show you were here, your social security number to get your check on the first and the fifteenth and your death certificate so the jigga' that killed you can officially get his street cred. Sonja lives in the projects of Kleevland Ave. This area of town is referred to as 'one dead no witnesses', average life expectancy is the amount of time it takes a jigga to reload. It could easily be called Kleevland Ave Penitentiary for all the ex-convicts, parolees and wanted suspects running the joint. Kleevland Ave holds another distraction for me. It's where my friend and fellow recruit Michael Knight was gunned down.

Michael and I came up through the ranks together. He was doing undercover at Kleevland Ave. Posing as a low level drug connect, he flashed a bankroll, had old ladies fixing him meals and was fucking this chick named Peaches. It's been said, don't eat and fuck where you shit; it's true. Michael let his guard down. Turns out Peaches was fucking everybody, literally and figuratively. Sitting in his car in the parking lot completing a transaction of a ten-dollar piece of crack, Michael was caught slipping when the jigga' snatches the rock then puts a pistol to the back of his ear and fires. Michael was dead when the cops and paramedics arrived but they still had to pry his hand from the steering wheel.

Peaches set him up to get jacked by another jigga' she was fucking. When that Jigga' was busted for a gun violation he ratted Peaches out cause he heard she was fucking another Jigga' while he was locked up. As I drive up Division Street towards Kleevland Ave entrance along its eight-foot high iron fence that runs around the entire complex, there they are, gathered around the entrance sitting on milk crates and tree stumps. The hood sentinels who keep watch like jackals for anything weak or vulnerable to come along, but also sound the alert when 'the man' is rolling through. I rolled up in the black truck with dark tinted windows and bullet holes in the hood and side. I stop at the entrance then get out of the truck and walked around to the pack. I hit the big jigga first and tell the rest to sit down. That's for Knight, don't ever forget him! They coil up but don't strike. They know my reputation.

I get back in the truck then drive through the maze of two Story red brick buildings that sit on dirt lots that I'm sure had grass at one time. There were old cars with no tires or rims sitting on concrete blocks and broken bicycle parts thrown all over. Clothes lines across the courtyard with laundry drying, old people and small children are sitting on the porches and stairs hoping for a savior or at least a winning lottery number. Young women spend the day mingling around the apartment buildings, no one ever told them working a pussy is not a real job.

I roll past four young black men pulling the seats and sound system from a new Acura TL, I don't think they're pimping out the ride. Then I pull the truck into a parking space near apartment building number three and check my watch it's 10:15 am, I walk the cracked sidewalk to the stairs then up to the corner apartment 3C. Coming up the stairs I could hear loud conversation. When I reached the second level, I could tell it was coming from Sonja's apartment.

Before I could reach out and knock on the door it burst open. There was Sonja Wearing an oversized white t-shirt with a big picture of Mickey Mouse on the front and a pair of powder blue house shoes. She was yelling full throttle at this dude who was backing out the doorway. A dark skinned brother about 5'5" tall and 240 pounds with a fu-man-chu mustache, wearing a white chef's uniform with white shoes. Not sure who I am or why I'm at the door he looks confused as to whether he should run or walk pass me.

"Get your ass on way from here," Sonja shouts. He says, "Excuse me," as he shuffles by...then down the stairs.

"I can't believe that little cheap ass bowling ball Negro," Sonja says to me. "I've let him come over here and fuck me four times on credit then when I tell him I need rent money he tells me he ain't got it. He got nerve enough to come over here with a bag of grilled cheese sandwiches and tell me he can let me hold forty dollars. You aught to see that lil' dick he got, I'm doing him a big favor. Believe me, at forty dollars, I'm charging him ten dollars and inch, I ain't no gold digger, but I ain't trying to fuck no broke jigga either." Sonja then laughed with a big loud burst.

"Well, if it ain't the black private dick that's a sex machine to all the chicks, so what you doing here C.J.? You want to finish off the rest?" Sonja asked as she pulled up her t-shirt to flash me her naked body. "Come in and have a seat. It's good to see a brother around here whose money is longer than his dick". She walked over and sat on the living room sofa while I closed the door then came over and sat to her left. "In that sharp black suit you're not here for sex. Either somebody died or somebody's gonna be dead. Which is it?" Sonja asked.

"It's both, Slick's dead and I intend to kill the Three Blood Beast that did it, an Albino, African and Black Dread, three young jiggaz in an old car. Give me a scent so I can track them Sonja."

"C.J. you know I don't do young jiggaz if I can help it. I haven't fucked anybody like what you described. I'm sorry it was Slick; I know he was your best friend. Sit back and let me fix you something to eat."

"Thank you Sonja, but I feel like death has served me the scorpion, viper and cyanide special. My only antidote for this Frankenstein, Werewolf, and Blackula trio is revenge."

"These demons have brought the apocalypse now but I've started their tribulation period and this will only end with them being sent to hell."

"True enough," Sonja responded, "but you haven't had desert."

"I don't have time Sonja."

She stood, "Give me three minutes. There is always time for desert." It was less than three minutes the time she took to microwave a slice of apple pie on a small plate. Sonja then scooped on two golf ball size lumps of butter pecan ice cream. She brought that to the living room with a large spoon then sat next to me as I politely ate. She also had with her a tube of white hand lotion. "When the pressure's been on, you've brought me relief and I want to do the same for you." Sonja opened the tube and squeezed a hand full into her right hand then placed the tube in her lap. With her left hand she unzipped my pants and reached between my zipper and through the flap of my boxer shorts. She pulled out a fist full of cock, and then grabbed it in her right palm.

"You got a problem with this ghetto love?" Sonya asked me.

"I'd be the last one to throw the first stone baby, I know about all the hypocrites out here who criticize random pleasure and say romance must come before-play, but if I wasn't the real deal I could not run these streets. I got to be able to run up on a man reach into his chest and snatch out his heart then walk up on a women whistle and make my dick stand up and bark. In the hood ain't no time to play, all you need is a three inch slit, a hard ass dick and a brother that can pay, fuck what anybody else say. Now I'm going to finish this ice cream while you handle your business."

It was warm, creamy and full of nuts. The pie and ice cream was good too. She had a feathery touch like a bus station pick-pocket. Her stroke was smooth like a Michael Jordon jump shot. Before I knew it I had licked my plate clean and thrown it across the room. I was about to let go an ounce of fourteen karat sperm bank gold and wanted to tell her to point the barrel away from her face but my tongue was tide around my tonsil. I tried but the words wouldn't come. They were the only thing that wouldn't come. Then I bust in her eye with the egg yolk. But she was a pro. She used her free hand to scoop her face clean then asked me if I needed a warm wash cloth? I told her no, but thanked her for tightening me up. Sonja tucked my limp dick meat back gently into my boxers.

"Big dick, big balls, big money, you're a bad boy Lil Bond and that's where you should check."

"Where's that?"

"Badd Boyz Barber Shop, it's where the big dick, big balls, big money boys hang out."

"Oh really"

"Yes, all these cool cats want the latest cuts. Check for Vernon, he owns the joint, from Jacksonville to Atlanta, even Savannah. He's the king of the clippers. He's got a brother named George who's known on the street as 'DJ Rover.' George sets up and DJ's hooker parties for the type of young big balling thugs and hustlers you're looking for. They're paying big money too. I've tried to get in on it but they say I'm too old."

"No, they didn't!" I say in jest to Sonja.

"Yes! she responds, they all over yahoo but I can't get a yoohoo, hell, my gynecologist just told me two weeks ago I had the uterus of a twenty-five year old and the titties of a thirty year old. If they don't believe me, I can get fifty dudes here in Jacksonville to co-sign on that."

"Sonja, I'd be the last to doubt that but I got to go, me and Slick got a date and I can't be late." "Thanks for the tip," I said as I pulled a roll of hundreds from my front left pocket. "How much is your rent?" I asked Sonja.

"I need about six hundred to cover all this bullshit," she said. I peeled off a thousand and put it in her palm. "What about the extra four hundred?" she asked me. I told her to show herself the kind of love she just showed me. "Thank you C.J."

"Thank you baby for your time, you've been so much more than kind". I opened the door then stepped out.

"You stay strong and keep coming," Sonja yelled as I walked down the stairs to my truck.

I drove to the cemetery hoping the whole way Jesus would come there and raise my friend from the dead and forgive me in advance for what I was going to do when I found the Albino, African and Black Dread.

CHAPTER 9 – SOME PERFECT MOMENTS

I T'S A NICE day for a funeral, for someone other than Slick, I thought as I drove up through the gates of Magnolia Cemetery.

The Sun was shining, about 70 degrees and no clouds. Slick's family had decided on a graveside funeral even though his father had put aside all his drunken, hell raising ways and joined the Methodist Church, yeah, a deacon and even singing in the praise choir. After years of abusing his family and putting them through hell, he was good enough for church but Slick wasn't.

You roll through those gates and something real serious comes over you. Azelya's, fern bushes, palmetto plants around the feet of old oak trees draped in moss. It's a humbling reality strolling amongst the acres of marble head stones. They're men and women a whole lot badder than me laid out in this dirt. Brothers and Sisters who had a fearlessness; I'll never know. But I've been given one thing they'll never get, one more day to make things right.

The tent, the covered folding chairs, the outdoor carpeting positioned neatly around the pre-dug hole. The cemetery attendants who go about their business in a polite and professional way that suggest they've been expecting us for some time. They've known our entire life would culminate into this moment. Nothing we could do or say would keep us from ending up here. From the womb of our Mother to the womb of our Mother Earth and in between we write our Obituary. We're not issued the total value of our life until we are dead. Slick's life was priceless and the Albino, African and Black Dread are going to pay.

I pulled my truck up behind one of many cars that lined the long road through the cemetery. There must have been forty five or fifty people there. Slick and the family had not yet arrived. God I swear if it would change Slick's fate I'd go the rest of my life and never be late.

Still, more people came, dressed in black, brown, white, blue, pink and purple. There's no such thing as color restrictions for a black funeral. In the hood a funeral may be your only opportunity to get dressed up and go out to see old friends. Notice of a funeral in the black community is the equivalent of receiving and invitation to a family reunion. Classmates reunite, old people take a count on who's still left and baby mama's can check on whether their dead beat baby daddy has a new suit or car. As I walked across the field of graves to Slick's tomb, I approached the crowd gathered around the tent and chairs. I see many people from the neighborhood I have not seen in years. Elementary school teachers, church members and officials, high school class mates and many of our community leaders; Deacon Mc Dower, Deacon Kiser and Deacon Foster. In case you wonder? After years of hell-raising, if they're still alive, all black men become Deacons in the church before they die. Very few old saints are left standing in the 'gap', the new church people came and made God a parking lot attendant. They praise themselves and pray that God will forget they murdered their neighbor, neglected their children, cheated on their spouse with the choir director then ask God to bless them with a new Mercedes. Tina's there, her husband left her with five kids after thirty years, he got caught standing in the gap between Ms So-and-So' legs. Coach Wilbert was there, the first black football coach in the Orange Park. All them, bad ass, fine ass black women that kept young brothers around the neighborhood hard were there; chicks named Tricia, Rosemary, Dee Dee and Daisy May. But you can't go to a black funeral and not see them Jiggaz who you can't believe are still alive, those brothers that drink, smoke, get high all day and night, they've never taken a vitamin or eaten a salad in they're life. They have not exercised since the last time they were in jail and don't use protections during sex and will fuck anything from a bow legged beat up prostitute to a sheep. They're looking better than anybody. Walking advertisements that working for Satan may not pay that bad. I approach the crowd and sifted my way through meeting and greeting. In mid-conversation the entire crowd went quiet and heads turned in one direction. The lavender colored hearse carrying Slick's body followed by two limousines with the family and friends arrived. As the limousine came to a stop on the service road closest to the grave site, I moved quickly to the rear of the hearse to be the first to grab the casket. I hadn't checked to see if I was listed as a pallbearer but nobody was going to move that casket without me. The driver and passenger of the hearse exited and came to the rear door. The older well-dressed gentleman on the passenger side identified himself as H.W. Williams, funeral director and the younger man as Jr. With the rear hearse door open, Jr. stepped in the middle of two rows of men that have now formed. As Jr pulls the casket out the rear, I grab the long handle and pass it down to the next man until we all are holding our section, four men to each side. As we pivot and turn the casket to our right, Slick's parents, brothers and sisters emerge from the two limousines and follow us as we march the casket to its tomb. We reach the hole and rest the casket on the metal gurney that will lower it when the time comes.

While the family was being seated a small chorus of three women began to sing (In the Sweet By and By) and many in the crowd began to sob. Slick's sister cried heavy and went limp. Several women in the crowd moved close to her chair and began to fan her. H.W. Williams stepped to the front near the family and introduced the Reverend W.F. Grant Sr. who had elegant words that began with Bible scripture of John 14:3, And if I go and prepare a place for you, I will come again and receive you unto myself, that where I am, there ye may be also.

When he was done I was totally surprised when Slick's mother stood and asked me to come forward and say something as his best friend. As I walked up and stood in front of the casket to address the crowd, I felt a real peace come over me. I told them Slick was not perfect but he had some perfect moments.

"Isn't that just how God works it, allowing our imperfection to collide with the right opportunity? Then God manifests His greatness by transforming that collision into the perfect moment. Slick's life was one long Perfect Moment. He was the friend that God sent me. In God's own wisdom he's decided to take him back. I'll see you again, Slick, I'll see you again."

Someone in the crowd began to sing a chorus of the Negro spiritual 'Soon and Very Soon.' The entire crowd joined in. 'Soon and very soon we're going to see the King, soon and very soon, hallelujah, hallelujah, we're going to see the King.' The reverend then announced the conclusion of the service and excused the crowd. People then began to mingle and hug but very few left. After about fifteen minutes the grounds crew came and began the process of burying Slick. By loosening the belts of the gurney, they lowered the casket into a metal container that was suspended over the hole. Once the casket was in that container, a metal cover sealed it and that was lowered to the bottom of the dirt grave. The ground's crew then dismantled the equipment. Then a small tractor came over and pushed the dirt into the hole.

Several people in the crowd came forward and grabbed a handful of dirt and tossed it in the hole. Once it was full, the tractor packed it down. It was then I knew it was over. Even if Jesus Christ came and brought Slick back to life he still would not be able to get him up out of that hole.

CHAPTER 10 – I'M COMING ROSA

I LEFT THE CEMETERY and hit Interstate Ninety-Five South, somebody's got to tell me something or I'm gonna start hitting people in the mouth.

I headed straight to the Baymeadows area of Jacksonville on the south side of town following up on the tip from Sonja. I'm going to Badd Boyz Barber shop to talk to Vernon. I need a hook up not a tape up. I knew on any given day you might find one or two crime spree suspects hanging with the Brothers at the Barber Shop. It's important that you know who's who though, because most are loud mouth, mean mugging posers. These Guys have groomed themselves to be street tough from rap music and video games but are generally antisocial, immoral ass-holes. They sit around all day rapping about the smoke from the barrel until they get hit with the smoke from the barrel, the mourning wakes everybody up.

You'll find Blacks, Puerto Ricans and Whites lined up waiting to get their hair cut. Fades; ballies; tape ups; edges; and all the latest hip-hop styles.

Anything else you want that the streets offer you can get there too. They got caps, t-shirts, sneakers, jeans. They've got hair products, CDs, DVD? You want a stereo system, flat screen TV, a car? You want weed, crack, pussy, you want a jigga killed? You name it; this is where you can get it. Today I need information.

I walked in the door at Badd Boyz and the place was full, about seventeen or eighteen people. You wouldn't need but one guess to know which barber was Vernon. The first chair on the right, he's the one with

51

all the bling and talking the loudest. He's cutting a white guy's hair while talking on his cell phone and arguing with another barber about who's the greatest rapper…Biggie, Jay-Z or Naz. You also can't miss his oversize diamond belt buckle that read's VERNON. I asked myself, what really is up with these white guys chasing this thug style, hanging round barber shops and basketball courts talking all foul. They go to black clubs, listen to black music, always carrying a gun, saying they're just chill'n but the whole time scared one of them jiggaz might kill him.

"What's up CSI?" I know you and your reputation, Vernon said as I stood just inside the doorway. All the brothers around the shop stopped to check me out.

"Why you calling a brother out like that?" I asked him.

"Well, word is you never lost a case."

"I just catch them, I don't convict them."

"Word on the street is before you got plucked, you were judge, jury, and executioner." I checked my hair in the mirror and smiled. "How come you ain't no cop no more?" Vernon asked me.

"It's the cards you're dealt sometimes," I replied.

"Oh, yeah?" he asked. "Yes," I replied.

"My dude said you fucked some rich white woman in more ways than one. You really wrecked a car with some doctor's wife in it? That shit's bananas."

"That's kind of personal," I said.

"Well, we get personal up here in the barber shop."

Vernon was plucking at me like a mocking bird at a chicken hawk. "Why you think they call the barber shop the black CNN?" Vernon asked. The fellows in the shop burst into laughter.

"Well, check this, I said, I got breaking news for you. I'm looking for George." That drew some serious glances from the group.

"George who," Vernon asked.

"Your brother George," I replied.

"Oh yeah?" he asked.

"Yes," I answered. At that moment the only noise was that of some rap music playing in the background. Vernon stopped cutting the customer's head and stood facing me while rubbing the head of his clippers.

"Are you trying to put my brother in the obituary? You think my brother is some sort of snitch? You think my brother knows something about all these jiggaz getting killed in Jacksonville?"

"No, I replied, but he might know where I can find a dangerous trio: an Albino, an African and a Black Dread." "Unless someone here knows", then everyone in the shop either turned or looked away from me.

"Hell, C.J.! you ain't even no real police no more," Vernon said.

I looked hard into Vernon eyes and told him, "then it was a job, now, it's personal". "I'm just hoping George can help me follow up a lead."

"A lead uh?" Vernon asked with skepticism. Then he asked me if I knew the cost of a hair cut and shave?

I asked, "What is the cost?"

"With a tip from a really good customer it's a hundred dollars," he said.

This was Vernon's way of charging me for information. Okay I said, then pulled a hundred dollar bill from my pocket and put it on the counter next to Vernon's barber chair. He stopped cutting and took a long look at me before speaking.

"Stop by the Putty Cat Lounge about midnight and ask my brother your questions," Vernon said. At the same time he opened up his barber's smock to reveal a pistol in the waist of his pants. "But if anything happens to my brother, you'll answer to me." I nodded in agreement then turned and left.

I walked away from Badd Boyz wondering what price Satan paid for the souls of the young men inside, without Jesus businesses like these are becoming sleeper cells for Hell. God will deal with evil men however I will deal with the men who brought evil to me. I pulled out of the parking lot thinking of the dark path I would have to travel to find Slick's killer. It would be like chasing a cobra through the woods at night. Every step is danger and every strike is lethal. Little did I know the snake might be chasing me.

My cell phone rang. It was Rosa. She's hysterical, crying, short of breathe. "C.J. Come quick, please come quick!. I'm at the gallery."

"Baby, what is it?" I asked her.

"Yes, please hurry, J."

"I'm hurrying, Baby!"

"The police want to ask me more questions. I have to go." Then she hung up the phone, my foot pushed down hard on the gas peddle. I raced up San Jose Boulevard towards downtown Jacksonville. Running red lights, zipping through school zones, flying over railroad crossings, within a matter of minutes I was crossing over the Main Street Bridge into downtown. I caught the light cycle just right. The eighteen to twenty minute ride had taken me just eight minutes. An unmarked police car and two black and whites were parked in front of the Ninth and Main Restaurant and Art gallery.

I was up on the side walk and five yards from the door when the truck stopped and I jumped out. Through the front door you step into the bar and lounge with the dining area to the right or art gallery and social area to the left. I snatched the art gallery door open.

"Rosa!" I yelled as I walked quickly past a uniformed police officer standing inside the door. "Rosa!" I yelled louder. The gallery has large rear doors that open onto a concrete court yard with wrought iron table and chairs, potted plants and a large fountain in the center. The club itself was a favorite hangout of the urban hip. The open mic poetry types harmless enough, but it sat on a corner where crime was common. Rosa doesn't mind giving hand outs and leftovers from the restaurant. I believe because of a few people's goodness, God says, "Hey, I think I'll give this world another day." Rosa is one of those people.

I walked through the art gallery full of African, African American, Caribbean and Hispanic paintings and sculptures. I reached the far left of the building with its narrow hallway to her personal office. Six paces down on the left another uniform cop stood attention at Rosa's office door.

"I'm here for Rosa," I said as I reached the open door. There she was, seated on a small rollaway chair. In front of a desk covered with stacks of folders and two laptop computers, there was very little space in the room for all the boxed up paintings and sculptors yet to be opened. Holding tissue in both hands with her head hanging over facing the floor, her black big barrel curls hung down around her face. Even in distress she was sexy. Dressed in a sleeveless hot pink blouse, with sexy boot cut blue jeans and four inch mary jane pumps.

I knelt close to her chair. She looked up at me then threw her arms around my neck. I wanted to ask her what happened but I couldn't breath. I loosened her grip then pushed the hair back from her face. Her neck, face and eyes were puffy and red. I had only seen Rosa as the beautiful woman with the hot body and sultry voice. I had never imagined her hurt or in pain such as this. To my left, one standing and the other leaning against the wall are two plain clothed Detectives, both facing Rosa. It was them again, Bennie 'Big Biscuit' Bradley and Joe 'Jelly Bellie' Jackson. Biscuit and Jelly, they've solved about as many cases as Ronald McDonald and Burger King. "Officer Bradley, Officer Jackson," I spoke showing respect for their badges.

"He was going to kill me," she said.

"Who, Who Rosa" I asked her while stroking her hair and looking for his description in the terror in her eyes. "He's African," she said. So many terrible things went through my mind at that time. Could it be just a coincidence? Could this be the same African? An African killed Slick, tried to kill me and now attacks Rosa. It's got to be the same. There's a lot of Africans in the world, but not a lot in Jacksonville. Not a lot in Jacksonville fucking with me and my life.

"Tell me what happened, Rosa."

"I was showing art work;" she said.

To the African; I asked?

"No, this was a really professional looking white guy with extremely blue eyes who'd driven up in a black big body Benz. He came up right after I arrived. I told him the restaurant didn't open 'til three but he only wanted to see some art. I showed him some paintings and sculpted pieces. He said he liked what I had but was looking for a piece similar to one that was stolen from him. I then walked him to the door and watched him leave. I left the door and walked back to the gallery. As I came in, he must have been behind the door. He jumped me from behind and wrapped his right arm around my neck then pulled me to the floor. I tried to scream but he was on top of me choking me with both hands."

"Did he say anything?" I asked her. "He said he thought I was tasty and worth a trade but he had a job to do and I must die. What does that mean?" Rosa asked me.

"I'll get to the bottom of it." I told her. "But then what happened? How did you get away?"

"First, I struggled, but the more he choked me I began to beg for my life. Then there was a knock on the court yard window. One of the homeless men seeking handouts could see him holding me to the floor. He began banging on the glass and yelling as I felt I was loosing consciousness. The African jumped up and ran out the rear door and through the courtyard."

I turned to the officers and asked if they had gotten all that. "We've got her statement and the statement of the guy who ran him off," said Detective Jelly Bellie. "He told us the guy ran down the street and jumped into an old black hearse then drove off." "A Hearse," I asked. "He said it looked like an old hearse," Detective Big Biscuit said. "What is it with these old cars and do you have anything on Slick's case, yet?" I asked the detectives. Biscuit and Jelly told me they were aware of the similarities and were busy buttering up leads in search of information.

"Do you want us to call rescue for you, Ms. Rosa?" Detective Biscuit asked. "No, I want to rest in my own bed tonight and I might see my own doctor tomorrow."

"We've got a crime scene evidence unit coming to check for fingerprints and DNA. You can leave when they're done but we would like you to come by the police station to look at some mug shots." Rosa endured the process. All the evidence was collected. I thanked the officers for their help but told them Rosa and I would come by the station when she recovered.

I lead Rosa out of the building to the passenger side of my truck then reclined the seat then helped her in and closed the door, I walked around, got in and cranked the truck.

Rosa lay on her side facing me as I let music from the smooth Jazz station play. Rosa's eyes closed and I drove her home. The physical and emotional drama of the day had Rosa asleep the entire twenty two minute ride to the River Road apartment. Rosa must have sensed she was home. Her eyes opened and she sat up then reached for the door handle before I could get around and open the door. I held her door while she got out then we walked up the sidewalk to the apartment together. I opened the door then she stepped in ahead of me. A brush of her hair and rush of her perfume and a wave of passion came over me. With some of my doggish ways, I'm reluctant to put a label on our relationship. I should hold on to her tight and never let her go but men can be as fickle as women in matters of the heart.

"I'm going to start you some hot tea then a warm shower", I told her. Rosa walked to the bedroom while I prepared the herbal tea. I went to the bedroom and Rosa was sitting on the edge of the bed. I knelt down and removed her shoes. "C.J., that guy was trying to kill me," Rosa said. I could still hear bits of sorrow and fear in her voice.

"Rosa, I'll get to the bottom of this and people will die, but trust me it won't be you, you'll live forever. I won't allow anything to happen to you. You were there when I needed you. Knowing my record of relationships with women, you didn't hold it against me."

"When I was a young woman, C.J., my brothers and uncles told me a man could not be satisfied with one woman. So it is, what it is, or as they say in Puerto Rico, sun don't shine, then sun don't shine." Then Rosa put a hand on each side of my face as she softly kissed my lips. I had both her shoes off and was walking to the bathroom to start her shower when she asked me, "C.J., how do you know someone is going to die in this situation?" I stopped and turned to answer her, "Someone is going to die because I'm going to kill them."

Then I started her shower and she came into the bathroom wearing just her panties and bra. She took both off and handed them to me. Then Rosa pulled her hair back and twisted it into a ball and stepped into the shower. I left the shower curtain open enough that my eyes could indulge in its lust for her flesh. The slope of her spine, the curve of her waist, the perfectly crafted mounds of her ass, as sweet as anything I've known with her beautiful caramel tone. She slowly turns and the soap runs the length of her body like ice cream down the side of a sugar cone. Creamy suds dripping over her dark nipples, flowing down her smooth stomach then through her dark fine bush to the center of her thighs and down her legs. No cruise ship could offer a more pleasurable voyage. The design of a woman is the universal testament that there is a God. I closed the shower curtain and placed her underwear in the hamper. In the bedroom, I opened her panties drawer and took out her light pink camisole with the matching bikini panties. I placed them on the bed before going to the kitchen to get her tea. It took me four or five minutes to prepare a cup of Chinese imperial green tea and returned to the bedroom.

Rosa was already out of the shower and toweled dry. She didn't bother putting on the camisole and panties. She had pulled back the bed sheets and was lying naked on her stomach. I walked around to her side of the bed where I placed the tea on the night stand then lifted a bottle of scented body oil Rosa kept on the stand. I opened the bottle and slowly poured a small stream of oil down her spine into the crack of her ass. I poured a small amount in my hands and started to gently massage her neck and shoulders. She didn't open her eyes but a smile rose up on her face. I wanted us both to forget the events of the day. For this moment, make it all a dream. I slowly rubbed the oil around and down her back, over her booty and between her thighs. I put a little more oil into my hands and rubbed the back of her thighs, calves and feet. Without a word being said she rolled over onto her back. I took the bottle of oil and held it high then poured a couple of large drops on each nipple then poured a small stream from the breast to the belly button, from the belly button onto the pussy. I placed the oil on the stand then softly cuffed both breast, massaging them in slow circular motions with both hands circling the titties, the stomach, and the thighs. I sat on the bed near her feet to rub the inside of her thighs. When I did, she lifted her left leg around me and scissored me between both thighs.

I lifted her right leg and place it on my left shoulder and began to softly kiss the inside of her calf, then snake tongued down the inside of her thigh and just like I learned in biology class, calf meat connected to the thigh meat and the thigh meat is connected to the pussy meat. Then a big fat wet kiss but not too hard and not too deep, its not the hole you're working but the lips and the clit, unlike an ear of corn you don't eat down to the cob. She began to quiver the way you do when someone drops an ice cube down the back of your shirt. She's got large hands for a woman of which she palmed the back of my head in her right hand. The way Allen Iverson palms the basketball on his killer crossover. My head was locked into the rhythm of her pelvic thrust and I had her clit ringing like Ant Bee's dinner bell calling Andy and Opie. All the muscles in Rosa's body tightened and started to jolt like I was hitting her with a Jacksonville police stun gun.

I teed off on her ball and placed myself tight to the hole, all that was left was a tap in birdie. She moaned then gasped for air and screamed C J so loud all the neighbors know my name, uumm! pussy pie and here cums the whip cream. After a long exhale, she went limp and wet. She slid her right leg off my back and I lifted my head and took a deep breathe. I rolled her onto her right side and pulled tight behind her then spooned her to sleep.

CHAPTER 11 – PUTTY CAT

AFTER A FEW hours of sleep it was time to creep, my body, mind and soul told me to get my ass up and make shit happen.

I pulled my private number for Sheriff Max Bell. Max Belle is the toughest sheriff Jacksonville has ever had. He's a tough country boy out of Mayo, Florida via the University of Florida. U of F taught him criminology but I taught him the city streets. My time on the force taught me that to be effective and successful in this crime fighting business you must build your own coalition. Any time he had some menace to society he couldn't reach with the long arm of the law, he could call me to reach them with the long barrel of the gun. Max will still take my calls and do me a solid when possible. I got him on the phone and he quickly arranged for a uniform officer to stake out Rosa's apartment while I chased the bad guys.

Vernon was right when he said I wasn't a badge carrying cop anymore. What he doesn't understand though, is the badge didn't make me a cop. God gave me the gift for the job. That stuff that superman, batman and James Bond have in imaginary life, I have in real life. I prepared a fruit plate of apple, bananas, grapes with yogurt and another cup of tea then placed it on the night stand for Rosa.

I took a quick shower and pulled out my night running gear. A black Louis Vutton long sleeved shirt with black Dolce and Gabbana single breasted suit and a pair of black leather Berluti, string tie shoes. Top it off with a black Akubra Fedora with a white gold Rolex and a splash of Marc Jacobs's men cologne, socks and underwear -optional. I don't know if someone will die tonight, but I know for sure I'm dressed to kill. I opened a small metal safe box I kept in the back of Rosa's closet and took out a 40 caliber pistol. I loaded it, took off the safety then put it in the top drawer of the night stand. If someone got passed the officer outside, I'd want Rosa to have a fighting chance. The time has come to put my mourning aside to find the ones who killed my friend and hurt my woman. A week ago, I knew no Africans. Today, I got an African all up in my shit. I'm going to find him if I have to take a safari through the Congo. Who even knew that Albino's still existed? Murderous gun slinging Albino's! Once I was dressed, I kissed Rosa on the forehead. "Snacks on the stand and the gun in the drawer," I told her as I walked from the bedroom.

A police cruiser was parked in front of my truck at the end of the walkway. I tapped on the hood as I walked between the two vehicles then waved at the officer and he acknowledged me as I pulled out heading for the Putty Cat Lounge. Its 11:50pm, I'm rolling like a midnight thunder storm, cool, black and ready to strike. My granddaddy used to tell me to be careful, for the devil is out after midnight. He'd say where ever you are after midnight either the devils there or he's on his way there. To survive the thugs, thieves and murderers you have to meet their bad intentions with a greater measure of bad intentions. The night you come with less will be your last. That type of drama is what draws men like me, to a life like this. Walking through the valley of the shadow of death and wanting to be the baddest ass in the valley.

The Putty Cat Lounge is a snake pit located on Jacksonville's Northeast side. Hooker st and east 63rd, referred to by the law enforcement as the last half mile before hell. It had once been a well kept neighborhood of row houses that have been over ran by young murderous jiggaz who call it the 'Bangum', if they said it to you it was usually with a gun in your face.

It is literally a dead end street that if you make a wrong turn onto, like a fly in the web that's your ass; you're in the trap. Home owners are allowed to exist there to provide refuge for these children of the blood sport. But there's a price to pay for dealing with the devil.

At the end of the dead end street is what was a community recreation center and a small church. The recreation center has been painted purple with black trim and decorated inside with Christmas lights. Add a DJ booth and disco ball and you have the Putty Cat Strip Club and Lounge.

The club's owners, Crow Dog and Pumpkin Pie are a couple of the Cities most murderous drug dealers. The agencies that regulate this form of entertainment don't have anyone brave enough or suicidal enough to come and inspect the place. Any given night somebody is shot or cut and that's just the dancers on stage. These thugs run this community like Hitler ran Germany. The small church across the street was once painted white and held sanctified fire and brimstone holiness services. It is now painted black with the number sixty three painted on the side. Now they call it the whore-tel and pimps and dealers rent out the pews to customers that pay to fuck the prostitutes and strippers. Poker and crap games are held in the pulpit. Crosses have been replaced with posters of Tupac.

This collective of thugs, low lifes, and misfits call themselves the 63rd street boys. Young men with eyes that don't cry and hearts that don't break, with souls their parents pawned to the devil long ago for one more high.

The piercing sound of sirens burst through my thought as two emergency rescue vehicles race past me. They turned right a few blocks ahead of me at 63rd and Hooker, my turn. I gripped the steering wheel a little tighter and sat up a little straighter in my seat. Then checked the slant of my hat and the grip on the 9mm glock I had holstered under the dash. I've arrived, 63rd and Hooker st, the gate to Sodom and Gomorrah. I made the right turn onto east 63rd and barely missed hitting the young clean cut officer dressed in black tactical gear. Black boots, black camouflage pants with black t-shirt and cap that had the word police written across the front. I stopped my truck. He looked directly in my eyes with his fiery stare, never blinking as he slowly walked from the front to the driver's window. He was not white, but he wasn't black either. I let down the window.

"Almost didn't see you," I said. "It's okay. I'm securing the outer perimeter. It's a mess down there."

There was a far eastern tone to his voice. There was something about his shape but I couldn't place his face.

"I'm investigating a case I told him and asked would I be able to park down near the club".

"Sure," he said, just don't block the emergency vehicles. They've got a pot full of bodies down there." I let up my window and drove on. Maybe he knew me, 'cause he never asked for my I.D. or badge.

The street was lined with police cars and rescue units. I wove my way down through emergency vehicles and parked as close as possible. All the action seemed to be centered at the Putty Cat Lounge. I pulled up behind a police car about thirty yards away, stepped out of the truck and immediately became a target of attention for the crowd gathered in the street. "Man, you sharp as a tact," a voice shouted out. Another yelled, "Hey! It's the black prince of the south, but ain't no party tonight."

"Why is that?" I asked.

"Cause he slaughtered everything up in there."

"He who" I asked. When I asked the question heads turned toward an elderly black man sitting on the porch of the house I was parked in front of. From his wooden chair he spoke slowly with the gargle of beer foam in his throat.

"It was the Po-Po," he said. The Police; I asked? "He was dressed like the police with eyes of fire and he slaughtered some bad mother fuckers up in there."

Not sure what to ask next, I started walking toward the Putty Cat Lounge. "So who you?" a voice from the crowd asked. "I'm the black super hero who comes in and takes down the bad guys," I replied. "Well, you be careful, the voice responded, cause all the other black super heroes that done come down here got fucked up". "Thanks," I said, then kept walking.

I walked through the crowd of mostly young brothers. Midnight is the time in the hood when you get the full impact of the numbers of lost black men. If I've seen one fake gold chain wearing, earring wearing, pants off the ass, hat turned backwards fourteen to twenty four year old I've seen a million. Promising young men who early in life were abandoned by a demolished family and social system, the product of too young and ill equipped mothers and fuck anything daddies. Daddies who provoke their children to evil because they don't spend any quality time with them unless they're good at sports and will somebody tell these bitches that a orange soda, pork skins and honey bun is not a well rounded meal; the kids are going to school twitching and flicking like the backup dancers in the thriller video. Parents who know the JSO, FHP, CIA and DEA but don't know one bitch on the PTA. But I can't get distracted. I came for the bad guy and many of these brothers ain't bad they just got bad luck to be ejaculated into this bullshit.

I approach the police tape around the front of the Putty Cat. A uniformed officer, who I'm not familiar with, approaches me at the tape and asked if he can help me. I ask him if he knew which detectives where working the case. He says, "Detectives Bennie Bradley and Joe Jackson are heading the investigation." Detectives Biscuit and Jelly, again, I thought. Either they're the best the department has these days or they're not taking these murders that seriously. "I'm a colleague of theirs and I have information vital to the case," I told the officer. "Hold one minute while I check inside," the officer said. He walked to the door, when he opened it Detective Jelly Bellie Jackson was standing just inside. "There's someone here to see you. Says he's got information on the case," the officer told Jelly Bellie. I lifted the tape and walked to the door. "I saw you speaking with a patrolman at the San Marco crime scene, then I read the report from the homicide at the old mill, then it was your girl that was attacked at Ninth and Main. Now you show up at this slaughter house. You must have a crystal ball or this is one hell of a coincidence."

"I believe in destiny not coincidence," I told Jelly. "I'm here to talk to the D.J. He might have some pieces to this puzzle. Can I see him?" I asked detective Jelly. "Yeah, I'll show him to you, Jelly said, although it might be more appropriate to say, he is pieces to a puzzle." "How do you mean?" I asked. He motioned for me to follow him as we walked a short hallway into the open club area.

"Now, if you can put these pieces together you should end up with a D.J. and about eight other jiggaz." Jelly said. In partaking this vision my body stiffened up straighter than a pillar of salt. Not even the murderous legends of Julius Caesar had ever sliced through an adversary the way someone had done here! Quarters, halves, eighth of men's bodies slashed and slung about the room. Legs, wings, breast and short thighs, it was a human Popeye's twenty four piece with guts and gravy.

"J, you were one hell of a cop while you were on the force but officially you got nothing to do with this, unofficially though, we could use your help." Humbled by Jelly's words, I could only say, "Thank you." We slowly walked through the room engulfed in the strong scent of piss, pot and poontang. The room lights were on, the disco lights also. There were broken tables, chairs and mirrors. Fingers sliced off hands, hands sliced off arms. There were parts of faces cut clean off and five pointed stars cut into their forehead. Clothing cut through without fraying the fabric. The eyes of corpses still open showing the terror that gripped the room. Blood sloshed throughout the room as if some abstract artist was creating a murder motif.

After a moment of taking it all in, my eyes looked to the writing on the stage mirror. In big bold letters written in blood, 'Never the righteous forsaken.'

"Yeah, looks like the killer left us a message," said detective Big Biscuit, who approached from a side room. "We're hearing the place was hosting a private party by a guest D.J. named George." "That's the reason I'm here. He's my contact for possible info on the Albino, African and Black Dread in Slick's murder. So far, he's the only lead I had." "Well, maybe when all these fingerprints and gold teeth records have been checked, some of your boys might be here. Lord knows, over the last five or six weeks someone has been making Jacksonville a lot safer place to live," Biscuit said.

What do you mean detective? "Well, someone's been clearing the books on our most dangerous criminals and their associates. Most have ended up just like this. "So you think there all connected?" I asked Biscuit. "I do, he said, but it hasn't got much press because the people at the top believe this guy is doing the city a favor. What you got dead on this floor is a bunch of raping, robbing, drug dealing, and mobbed-up murderers. Maybe this guy did do us a favor". "This guy, you think one person is responsible for all this?" I asked. "Our witnesses here tell us it was one man. They all say it was a police officer."

"I heard that on the way in, so what's that all about?" I asked. "Well, the witnesses say he came through the front door wearing black boots, black military combat pants with a black t-shirt and cap that had the word police written across the front of both. They say he was carrying a sword in one hand and a long blade in the other. Then he yelled some kung-fu shit before he went David Carridine on the whole fucking room, stabbing up jiggaz like a blood drunk vampire. He killed all the men and let the women go." I asked Biscuit if I could speak to the witnesses.

So, we stepped over the mutilated body parts to a side door that took us to the kitchen. It was the filthiest, nastiest, greasiest, grimiest kitchen I'd ever seen. There were three young women dressed in lingerie and high heels sitting at the table in the middle of the room eating boiled crab from a big pot. With Biscuit and Jelly on either side of me, we approached the table.

"So, you ladies want to give your name and tell us exactly what happened." "My name is Crystal," the girl in the middle spoke. "This is Pepper and this is Rashauanda," Crystal said introducing the girl to her right and left.

"So, what happened Crystal?"

"I'll tell you what happened. The Police ran up in here, told us to run then started killing every jigga in here."

"What else did you see?" detective Jelly asked Crystal. "What else I saw? I'll tell you. I saw the ass and elbows of the bitch running in front of me. I saw Rashaunda's backside. Damn that girl can run. She ran past all of us. They need to call her Run-Shaunda-run."

"That girl didn't outrun me", Pepper said. "I ran track against her in school." "Yeah, and she beat you then," Crystal said. "That was in ninth grade. I tore the heifer up in eleventh and twelfth grade year."

"You lying," said Crystal. "I ain't lying, you lying," Pepper said. "Don't you call me no liar, bitch," Crystal said.

"HEY! Hey! That's enough," said Detective Jelly, "Both of you stop talking." Then Rashaunda asked me if she could say something. I asked her what it was. "I'll out run both these whoes" she said and the three started to argue again.

CHAPTER 12 – CALL HER ROXY

I STAYED WITH THE detectives as they interviewed the witnesses. Body parts where collected and the crime scene processed. I watched as a headless body with the word George tattooed across the chest was tagged and bagged.

No matter how contrary a person may live, once they're dead you feel their life was worth something. Even these young men's lives that have been caught in this evil surge had the potential for joy and beauty. But had they all earned a death sentence?

Had George? I not only had killers to catch but George's brother, Vernon, to deal with now.

I won't let some reckless rampage killer destroy my city. He may feel justified because of who those people were, or what they did. All that being said, his personal justification does not equate to justice. Even though I want justice for Slick and Rosa, I will not destroy my community or city to get it. I lost my badge but not my love for J-ville. I'll hunt the evil that took Slick, that hurt Rosa and that did this barbaric deed.

Standing on the stage inside the Putty Cat Lounge, thinking over the killers words left on the mirrored walls behind the stage: 'Never the righteous forsaken.' He's got that right but what he didn't note was the fearless will step forward and evil will not prevail. Questions with no answers, mysteries with no clues, mothers and grandmothers left broken hearted, I let detectives Biscuit and Jelly know I would be by the station with Rosa later that morning. They told me it would take all morning to process the paper work from the crime and come up with a list of suspects. Could this be a vigilante cop? Could this shit be tied to what happened to Slick and Rosa? It's 3:00am and I've got too many thoughts to sort through for me to sleep. I crank my truck and decided I'll head over to Nubbie's restaurant. With the type of customers he gets coming in this time of day, I might spend a dollar and get someone to drop a dime.

I leave the club and slide my truck out to the corner of 63rd and Hooker, slow rolling like a long black snake night prowling for a life to take. The Albino, African and Black Dread might as well be one monster with three heads, I want them all dead.

I pause there and turn the music off. Under the full moon, I want to listen to the quiet of this time of day. The time of day when it's the darkest yet nothing goes unseen. Surely, I'm being watched. The streets are always watching. Maybe by the killer I'm tracking or maybe other opportunistic predators. 3:00am is a time when the human owls and foxes make their last run of the day. With the strip clubs closing and some of the pay by the hour motel guests wanting to beat the sunrise you have men cruising the streets who shouldn't be. Brother's riding in nice cars with fresh bills from the ATM, the fox looking to lure his prey into range then pounce; a family man straying, an out-of-town business man looking for some strange pussy or the guy who doesn't want to admit it but can't get it any other way. There's not much to choose from this time of day, no gold club dancers or hooters girls.

None the less, guys are trying to find someone with a three inch slit and a clit to knock off a nut. So, the hard luck beat up alcoholic or drug addict whoe from the trailer park don't look so bad. But beware, there owls out. Watching, waiting, don't slip up or get caught with your pants down. You barely notice him walking in the dark, trailing that trick on his bicycle. He's across the street smoking a cigarette under the light pole. He's strolling slowly down the side walk hoping someone will make the mistake of stopping to ask for directions. The moment your guard is down or you're too high or your dick's too hard to care, he'll attack with a knife to the neck, a bullet to the back. You were looking to get jacked off but you just got jacked! Some last chance, three strikes jigga fucked you up. The streets are always awake, don't get caught sleeping. The moral of all street wisdom is that you make sure you make it till tomorrow.

Bang! Bang! Bang! "What the..?"

"Hey!" she said.

"What the fuck!" I yelled as I realized she was just banging her hand against the side of the truck and not shooting at me.

"I scare you?" she asked in a loud raspy voice.

"You scared the fuck out of me," I responded before I even had a chance to think. All the while looking around before I let the window down. I never heard or saw her walk up from behind my driver's side window. Bad move on my part especially on this side of town. She motioned for me to let down the window. I put my left hand on the button then leaned forward and stuck my right hand under the dashboard and gripped the 9mm hidden there. I pushed the button and the window went down.

"What's up, playa?" she asked while poppin' some gum in her mouth and holding a cigarette in her right hand. "Damn, you clean boy. Who you, James Brown's nephew?

"So, what's up?"

"I must have been day dreaming. I didn't see you come up," I told her. "I scared you?" she asked.

"Maybe, maybe my senses ain't as sharp as they used to be," I said, the whole while checking the not so typical trick out. She was in her late thirties or forty something. A white chick, oval face, straight nose, thin lips and brown eyes about five seven in heels and probably a hundred and forty pounds, kind of thick legs, permed up shoulder length blonde hair and sunburned white skin.

She reminded me of a shift manager at Wal-Mart, but I hear from some prostitutes that it's hard to turn back once you realize you can get paid for a blow job. Still it ain't no secret though, if you buy that crack it'll have you selling your crack. She fits that type to me. "I'm looking for a party; you're dressed for a party, so let's party," she said boldly. "I told her I'm out more for business than for pleasure."

"Well, the only business going on this time of morning is pleasure, unless you're a cop," she said. "Not exactly, but I am looking to cop some information."

"I tell you what I know, playboy. I know you ain't gonna turn this down." At which time she took a step back from the truck for me to get a good look at her. She was wearing a navy blue tank style silk pull over top with no bra, dark grey linen slacks that zip up on the right side with a pair of dark colored closed toed heels. She reached her left hand across and held the waist band of her slacks then zipped the six inch zipper down. With her left hand she pulled the right side waistband down and with her right hand lifted her top above her chest, revealing to me her big lightning strike blue varicose veined titties with their pink nipples and baby powder white skin down to her panty-less pubic area. She's not a true blonde.

"Put in you order before I close up shop", she said. "Any hole you want, I also got something good to eat or do you want me to smoke on your swisher sweet."

I then thought how most of the people out on these streets living this life and running these games got here because somebody early on in their lives betrayed them, ran out on them and didn't live up to the obligation they'd made to them. I'm not here to exploit what a person feels is their last chance.

"So, what's your name," I asked her.

"Roxanne," she replied. "But you can call me Roxy."

"Well, Roxy, I don't know what brought you to this corner tonight, and don't misunderstand me, I respect the fact that no matter the cards you've been dealt, no matter how your luck's been running, you still handling your business. You're offering me all this pleasure and maybe another time or place. For right now, I'm looking for some dudes that been going around dishing out a whole lot of pain."

"Sounds like you looking to do somebody some harm," she said. "If it comes to that," I told her. "I want these brothers dead or alive, but you reap what you sow and they've sown death."

"Well, baby I feel your passion for what you're doing but if you don't want a fuck or a suck, how am I going to get paid?" "Help me get off on three young jiggaz, early twenties; a Dread with a gold grill and scar on the left side of his face, a real light skinned jigga, Albino and an African, straight Zulu with yellow eyes. I'm sure they run the street, tittie clubs, dope houses." "You seen them?" I asked Roxy.

There was a pause and Roxy looked hard into my eyes and said, "The Albino."

"The real light skinned dude," I replied. "The Albino," Roxy said as what little color she had seemed to drain from her like sand from an hour glass. "He crossed my path like a black cat walking on broken mirror glass under a ladder. He's one whacked out brother," Roxy said.

"So, he's strange?" I asked.

"I mean he's crazy," Roxy said in a firm voice.

"Even in this business there are some people you regret fucking. Doctors at the clinic say my asshole will never be right again."

"Tell me about him," I said to Roxy. "He picked me up one night driving some old dirty pick up truck loaded down with wood. The truck was dirtier inside than out and he was dirtier inside than out. He's about five feet ten or so. He had this sticky tree sap stuff all over him. He wore dirty work pants and steal towed boots. His afro and finger nails were full of dirt, but he had a nice muscular build. He didn't wear a shirt. You can tell he likes flashing his tattooed chest and arms. I told him my price and he pulled out a role of bills. He told me to get in then put the role back in his pocket. He bragged that he and his boys had just robbed some Mexicans so he wanted to celebrate. Everybody knows Mexicans carry cash so I figured he was good for it."

Roxy continued on telling me how the Albino drove her to the Gateway Motor Lodge. A place known around the north side of town as the 'Whoe Market', where whoes so broke and hard up they'll suck you, fuck you, wash and wax your car for a ten dollar rock and a five dollar tip. "After the Albino and I got to the room shit really got weird. I stripped off my clothes then sat on the side of the bed. He opened up a paper grocery bag he brought in with him. He pulled from the bag a stick man figure made of corncob and laid it on the old wooden dresser. He asked me what I believed in. I told him I believed in getting my money. He told me I would get what I had coming to me. Then he pulled a big fat joint and one of those flame thrower lighters from the bag and lit the joint." Roxy talked and I could hardly wait to hear what was next. "He took a couple of deep hits on the joint and blew the smoke on the corncob stickman. Then the Albino unzipped his pants and let them drop to his knees. He didn't have any draws on, but that crazy colorless Jigga had dick for days. He looked at me with the joint in his mouth then took out a large folding hook bill knife. He unfolded it using his left hand. I don't scare easy, but at that moment I was scared. He reached back into the bag then pulled out a little bitty baby chick that had its beak taped shut. Before I could gasp in horror he had already cut the baby chicks head off and was dripping small bits of blood on the corncob stickman. He placed the hook bill knife on the dresser and held the big joint in his mouth and took a huge draw from it. At the same time he leans his body back then his dick begins to rise and straighten like one of those long balloons at a clown party."

"I stand up from the bed and tell him to pay me. I'm out of here! The Albino straightens up, looks at me and pushes me back onto the bed. Before I could try to stand back up he scoops up both my legs one in each arm and pushes me further onto the soiled bed, never bothering to take off his pants or shoes. Kneeling on the bed he lifts my legs up against each side of his chest then moves up close and pushes his hard dick up in my pussy."

"That Albino mother fucker then drips the little bitty's blood all over me while he smokes that big ass joint and fucks me in the buck position for what seemed like hours, the whole time mumbling and talking to himself. When I told him I couldn't take it no more and begged him to stop, he pushed my legs down and rolled me onto my stomach then started fucking me in my ass with no lubrication. I struggled at times to get him off of me but he was strong as an ox. Once that psycho dick trip was over, I got dressed. He pulled up his pants. I asked for my money so he pulled out the roll of bills and threw it on the bed. When I counted the bills it was nine dollars. What kind of joke is this? I asked the Albino. He reached in his opposite pocket and pulled out a hand full of coins then threw that on the bed. It counted up to two dollars and eleven cents. "Give me my money you sick fuck!" I yelled.

"Before I could react he had grabbed me by the neck with his left hand and had the hook bill knife in his right hand. He slammed me against the wall, cut open my blouse and slit my right nipple. I was horrified and couldn't move or talk. He turned to gather his corncob stickman and left. I spent a month in the hospital with a torn rectum and busted hemorrhoids."

"Where can I find him?" I asked Roxy.

"I don't know, she said, but if you do find him stick something up his ass before you kill him."

"He will pay, he owes God, man and Justice; he will pay! I tipped Roxy two hundred dollars then drove off."

The scent of the Albino was in the air. Like high grade herb, his ass is grass and it's time for him to get lit up with hot lead!

CHAPTER 13 – THE ALBINO

AS I DROVE down Main Street, I felt even more urgency to solve these crimes. The Albino sounds like the kind of satanic bastard that would have enjoyed killing these east side boys tonight. No matter if it's eastside or westside, north or south. Somebody's declared it open season and their killing jiggaz like it's going out of style.

They must not have read Exodus 20 verse 13. Before I kill them I'll read it to them. Off Main Street, I catch MLK to U.S. 1 then Soutel Dr. to Nubbie's.

When I pull into Nubbie's restaurant and lounge at 5:00am, it could just as easily been 10:00pm. The lounge stops serving alcohol at 2:00am but folks still dancing, talking shit and sipping from their glove compartment stock in the parking lot. I step in the door to find all the usual suspects. There's Earl on a stool at the counter, Atlanta sitting in a booth with a table full of racing forms doing his daily handicapping and Can't-chance-it dancing in the middle of the floor to Jr. Walker and the All Star's tune, Shotgun.

The tune was being played loud from the jukebox where a fine young red bone was standing dropping in quarters and doing a sexy little booty dance. With long red hair, cut off daisy duke jeans, a white tank top and flip flops. She had everybody's attention.

As I walked up and took a seat at the counter, Nubbie rolled out from the kitchen in his wheelchair. "What's up, J., early morning or late night?"

"The way ya'll jamming it don't make a difference", I answered. "Let me have a large coffee." "Okay, you want a special with that?" Nubbie asked. "No thanks, but I am looking for some special information." Then Earl sitting at the right end of the food counter yelled out at me. "I need some information too." "Oh yeah, what you want to know, Earl?" "Look here," Earl said then asked, "if they repo your car, can they suspend you driver's license?" "No," I answered. "Well, then them KkracKers can kiss my ass. I ain't paying them shit." Nubbie sat my coffee on the counter and responded to Earl. What the fuck you talking about Earl? Before Earl could reply Atlanta in the booth next to the wall behind Earl spoke up. "I got a good one for you C.J. The eighth race of the matinee today; it's a sure thing, a cold lock. "You always say you got a lock", Earl said, that's how I got my fucking car repoed. I lost all my money fucking with you. "You got to trust your handicapper," Atlanta said. "You keep giving out that bad advice and somebody's going to make you handicapped," Earl yelled. "No thanks," I told Atlanta. "I need some different information. I need to know where I can find a crazy young psycho, albino jigga." Don't know him, they all replied. I don't know a lot of them young jiggaz, Nubbie replied. My nephew is in the back shooting craps. Go through the kitchen and out the back then ask for 'Boogie'.

As I stood from my stool with my coffee Can't-chance-it danced up in front of me. In a loud voice with his hands to the ceiling, spoke. "The sky is black, his skin is whiter than white, fire rises from the ground and it's raining judgment. Evil is going to burn, nothing will be learned. Police will still find no suspects at this time."

"Maybe this time you could come and watch my back," I told Can't-chance-it. "I would but it's dangerous out there and I can't chance it," he answered.

I walked around the counter and pushed open the swinging kitchen door. The kitchen was jumping. There was Nubbie's mother or mom's and her sisters, Ms. Mary Lee, Ms. Pearlie Mae, Ms. Lena Mae, Ms. Flora Mae, Ms. Mammie Lou and Ms. Maude all over pots and pans of grits, eggs, sausage and potatoes. Preparing the best soul food breakfast you could imagine. "Good morning" I said.

"Hey baby, moms spoke, you wanting some of this good ole breakfast?"

"I'm just passing through, but it looks and smells delicious."

"Here boy," taste this bacon said Ms. Mary Lee as I past her table. I took a slice of crispy bacon from her out stretched hand, two bites it's down. "Ooh that's good, but I'll be back for more." Well, you come on back we got plenty, said moms. "Thank you I will, then exited the rear door.

The door closed and it was all eyes on me. There were eight young jiggaz kneeling or standing under a light pole on the black top that circles the rear of the building. Jeans hanging with white tee's and tattoos. Menacing looks and piercing eyes. Nostrils expanded sniffing for fear. Young back males turned out by Satan while their parents are out praising. When you're young, strong, uneducated and high on weed and rap music...this is your life; stick up kids, carjackers, and triggermen. Teenagers and already married to this lifestyle. No pensions or 401k's in their futures. Ten, twenty, life and lethal injection are the contracts that they've signed. To make a long story short, the Ritilin didn't take. I tossed the coffee cup.

"Who you?" the littlest jigga kneeling with the dice in his hand turned and asked me. All the rest stopped and stood facing me. "I'm looking for Boogie." I told them.

"Are you 5-0?" The little jigga asked.

"You must be the spokesman for the group," I told him. Nubbie told me I could find him out here. What you want with him? Lil' dude asked again. I need some information. You need to call the phone company for that, he answered.

I moved closer to the group and pulled out a roll of bills and tossed a fifty on the pile of ones and quarters they were gambling over. "We could just take all that roll and leave you in the dumpster," short jigga said. Then with my right hand I lifted my right pant leg to reveal the 25 caliber I had holstered around my ankle. "Yeah you right my jigga, if the truth be told you got me out numbered and y'all could rush me like a prison break and I end up in the dumpster. But with sixteen in the cartridge and one in the hole, it's a lot more to that story to be told." They all step back. I knew then they were chicken, but I was out looking for beef. "You could do that, I told him or you could help me out and I'll make it worth your while without all the drama." Then I dropped another fifty on the pile. He paused then looked around at the other dudes who were apparently waiting to follow his lead. "What can I help you with?"

"I'm looking for a badass Albino brother, you know him?"

"I know him, but are you sure you want to find him?"

"I'm positive, I told him, he's left blood in the water now the shark is here".

"He's part of the voodoo zombies", Boogie said. "What's that?" I asked Boogie. "They're into all kinds of spells and witchcraft and mind fucking."

"Where can I find him Boogie?"

"The Woodpile"

"What?"

"The Woodpile on Phillips Highway, he cuts wood over there when he ain't out fucking people up." I dropped a hundred more on the pile, said thanks, then turned and walked away.

As I walked to the corner of the building, I stopped and looked back at the young men gathered in a circle arguing over how much each person's share of the loot would be. I turned the corner of the building and could hear foot- steps running up behind me. I turn to brace myself for what was coming. It was Boogie. "Yo, yo long money, hold up" he called out. "What's up?" I asked.

"Since you tight with Nubbie, I'll hip you to something."

"What is it?" I asked.

"Who you looking for, be careful; them boys in deep with the devil. That voodoo, witchcraft shit. Word is they turning jiggaz into zombies. I don't fuck with them. They're dangerous. Real dangerous"

"Thanks," I said, then turned and continued my walk to my truck. "Look me up, maybe I can help you with some more shit," Boogie yelled as I neared my truck.

Pulling out of the parking lot, I dialed Rosa on my cell phone. "I've been up all night, I won't make breakfast. I've got a hot tip that might lead me to the end of this trail of chalk lines, police tape and lost lives." I got onto I-95 south to Baymeadows Road then Phillips Highway south.

Two miles down, I passed it to make sure then turned around, not to alert. I pulled my truck off the side of the road about 100 feet and walked along the wooded roadside to the entrance of the property. This was an old family owned business that cut, chopped, sawed and sold wood year round, that along with salvaging old vehicles for parts. As much as a home business it was a compound. As I entered the property through a wide raggedy wooden gate the two acre property of sprawling woodpiles amongst what most people would call junk. Off to my left there was a family home. I walked a dirt road lit by 55 gallon steel drums full of burning wood with old Cadillacs, Pontiacs, and Ford cars on each side of the road. Cars so old there was mold growing on the rust. But mostly old pick-up trucks cluttered the property. Old dented, smashed up, broken down pick-trucks whose beds are loaded down with fire wood. There's fire wood everywhere. Anything that could hold or carry firewood did. The early morning fog and smoke from the barrels made visibility limited. I followed the road stepping light on my feet like an Indian scout looking for scaps. Continuing down the road, I came upon a small mountain of woodchips, mulch, and sawdust. Just then the fog and smoke were pressed back by a huge fire coming form a large pit.

The pit was easily twenty feet wide with a flame rising from ground level about five feet. I maneuvered around it and passed more cars stacked one on the other, some were four vehicles high. Then directly in front of me, standing at the top of a mountain of wood chips, ten or twelve feet high, it was him.

Standing there, as if he had been waiting his whole life for me, was the Albino. Sucking the last bit of life from a marijuana roach in his right hand while he rubbed his crouch with his left, he's got a huge bulge like his dick is hard. Chopping that wood had him ripped and cut, all muscle no gut

For a few seconds, I was gripped by the fear of the unknown. I quickly gathered myself. The light from the pit fire was shining on him, but God was smiling on me. Like a great warrior atop his woodpile kingdom, he stood.

His wooly afro was full of wood chips and sawdust. White skin covered with dirt and smoke film. Jeans so dirty, I can't make out the original color and a pair of lace up steel toed work boots. He did not wear a shirt but did have a Velcro back support around his waist. On his left forearm was a tattoo of a five-pointed star above an upside down cross, on his right forearm was a naked woman with her arms and legs spread.

We looked into each other's eyes with no words spoken, no declarations, no accusations, no threats. He had said everything at the old mill when he killed Slick and tried to blast me with that shotgun. We had irreconcilable differences and our association was going to die right after he did. I'm not under estimating him, but for any great story to triumph the evil Villon must die. He'll be difficult to take down, but I thrive on adversity. Then out of nowhere it starts to rain, ain't that bout a bitch.

Fuck it, I took off running up the wood pile at him and he came sprinting down towards me. We collided midway. I've done a lot of things in my day but falling and rolling down a mountain of wood chips wasn't one of them. Next time, I'll wait at the bottom till he comes down. Wood chips hurt!

But none the less we fought. We battled like two heavy weight boxers in the squared circle, like ninja warriors, like the evil spirit and the exorcist. He was striking me faster than a diamond back rattle snake and I was clawing back at him like a mongoose.

I started hooking off with jabs and upper-cuts, he started dipping and kicking with that kung fu stuff. Then he hit me with a left and right hook to the face, his knuckle game is nice too. I grabbed his right wrist with my right hand and pulled him past me and threw a side kick to his midsection. He twisted and blocked my kick then hit me with a backhand to the head. I threw an overhead right but he knelt down into a twist stand and blocked my hand with his forearms, then kicked me in the shin, mother fuck that hurt! He spun around and came up with a throat thrust which I knocked away with both arms. He turned to the side and threw a side kick with his right foot which I spun out to absorb the blow. Then, I hit him with a straight front kick.

He spun to his left, slipped my kick and grabbed my balls. Needless to say, that shit hurt. I stepped over his hand and with my back to him kicked backwards hitting him in the face. He lunged back into a backward summersault. My testicles felt like I had been boxing a ring full of leprechauns. I stumbled back and fell up against a stack of fire wood then grabbed one of the splinted logs and broke off a twelve inch spike of wood and charged at him. I lunged forward with the spike and he sidesteps to the left. I swung back across my body and he went down and rolled under my out stretched arm. I stabbed down at him and he sprung up and over my arm.

I charged at him with the spike and chased him to a column of cars stacked next to the pit of burning wood. As he neared the stack of cars, I lunged forward again, at which time he stepped up on one of the cars with his back turned and did a back layout over my head. I turned around and swung but he fell back onto the ground and kicked me backward with both feet into the column of cars. Then he sprung up to his feet.

With the spike in my right hand, I threw a punch towards his head with my left hand which he blocked with both forearms. Then he bitch slapped me across the left and right side of my face. I then swung my right hand with the spike which he ducked and used my momentum to turn me around and get his right arm around my neck. Oh fuck! As he attempted to choke and snap my neck I gathered my last bit of conscious fight and plunged the spike underneath my left armpit into his chest and heart, only with death do we part. I felt his grip loosen as he stumbled back. I turned to face him and fight, but dropped to my knees exhausted.

I could see life leaving his body with the stream of blood flowing from his wound. Holding onto the spike in his chest with both hands and laboring to deliver his last revelation. The Albino said to me, "It was you we wanted at the old mill not your friend, but we weren't going to get just you, but your family, too."

"But why bitch? Why?" I screamed for an answer from the Albino.

"An eye for an eye, tooth for a tooth, hand for a hand, foot for a foot and life for a life," he proclaimed. "You have vexed the beast and taken the jewel from the throne".

"What the fuck does that mean?" I asked the Albino.

"I run up on you with my chest all swole and you let the air out of me with this wooden spike, you've taken my life, he said, you must be a bad mother fucker." Those were his last words before he stumbled back and fell into the pit of burning wood. As I watched him slowly fall, I gave the Albino his eulogy.

Nightie night, sleep tight, you'll find hell the first turn on your right. Word says thou shall not kill, thus Justice and judgment have come to he that slay the innocent and murdered my friend, and for you too Roxy.

Yes, 'Justice' has come.

The rain stop, there was a small break in the clouds and a thin ray of light shined down over me. With that this chapter of my life was over.

CHAPTER 14 – STATUS

STILL AT THE pit on hands and knees, I didn't want to leave till I'd paid Heaven's fees. I pray oh God, I C.J. deliver this soul to your judgment today hoping it is for a just cause not merely for the revenge of my friend."

At that time I heard a voice calling, "Sir Sir?" I looked up to see a middle aged white gentleman in casual clothes. He appears to be a customer. "I wanted to buy some wood, but are you alright?" "Yes, I'm okay," I answered. "What is that burning in the pit?" He asked me.

"That? Oh that's the Albino. I'm holding his candlelight vigil." I could see fear in the man's eyes as he began backing away from me. The gentleman pulled a cell phone from his left pocket then I hear him say, police!

"You don't understand," I told him. "I have slain this monster to protect my people, the people of Jacksonville". As David slew Goliath to protect his people, I'm here to defend the children of J'ville from these evil and cruel bidders not simply to revenge my friend, with him still alive so many will never know another starry night or sunny day.

The man turned and ran towards the entrance. Just men know life should not be taken without a righteous cause or purpose unless the price of that life is charged to the taker in judgment. I bowed my head and continued my prayer. "Lord, oh Lord my rock, my fortress, my deliverer. God my strength in whom I trust. I wish to dwell with you forever. Thy rod and thy staff shall comfort me all the days of my life and Lord if I die before I next wake please send another to carry the long staff of righteousness or a long barrel pistol. Amen."

I had knelt near the heat of the pit and the smell of burning flesh for nearly ten minutes when the Jacksonville sheriff's department vehicles began arriving. I stood and slowly made my way to the front. Right behind them came detectives Biscuit and Jelly, all of them being directed past me by the gentleman customer.

I had stopped at the front gate when the JTA city bus stopped at the roadside bench, just right of the entrance. The bus' doors opened and on the steps of the bus stood a six foot chiseled face, lean muscular built man dressed in black. Black pants and t-shirt, black leather boots with a black skull cap and sun glasses. He was carrying a black grip bag. His silhouette could have been the same as the man I saw from Rosa's window or the cop I spoke to at 63rd and Main approaching the Putty Cat Lounge. He seemed apprehensive about stepping from the bus with all the police activity. He stood in the doorway even after the bus driver asked several times if he was getting off here. He didn't and the driver closed the doors and drove off. "C.J.! God damn you, C.J.! What the hell?" Phrases I hear coming from behind me that jolted my thoughts from the man on the bus.

I turned to see detective Biscuit rolling towards me. "What the hell do you think you are doing?" he asked. "You think you some one man police force? Hell, you ain't even on the police force. You were a good cop and I know you lost a friend, but I'm heading this investigation. I'm the engine that's pulling this train and if you want to add something you can hook on the caboose. How am I supposed to do an investigation with nothing but a burnt up corpse. Hell! That ain't even a corpse. It looks like a burnt slab of Jenkins' barbecue ribs, the thin end. I should pull you in and charge you with murder. Don't go from being a good cop to a bad prisoner." I nodded confirmation for what detective Biscuit had to say then spoke.

"I have nothing but respect for the job you have to do and the system you protect. Your job is to take evil men in and hope they will turn their life over to God. My job is to send them to God and hope the one behind him will turn his life over to God before I get him. If this means one less murder, one less robbery, so be it. The system builds security by forming steel and brick into more jails. I build security with the bodies of bad asses like this. This is my assignment from God, and I'm not leaving it."

"Bullshit! yelled Biscuit, C.J., How am I going to get the respect of these jakes if I let you go around killing and burning up everybody you think is a bad guy. You're starting to look like bad luck C.J."

"Hey! Hey there!" a voice called out. The detective and I looked towards the pit area. There I saw the biggest man I've ever seen in my life. He was about six feet four inches tall and at least five hundred pounds. He was a black man who appeared to be around forty years old. He had about a four inch afro and a beard about the same length. He was wearing overalls with no shirt and flip flops. He was holding the hand of a fat little boy wearing cut off jeans and tennis shoes, but also no shirt. The boy must have been eight or nine but looked like he weighted one hundred and sixty pounds.

"Hey, excuse me, I don't mean to interrupt yalls conversation," the big man said. "Who now gonna chop and chunk my wood?" "Sir, I take it you're referring to the deceased man," said detective Biscuit. "Deceased, no, I'm referring the man ya'll done executed by fire in my pit back there. He burnt up badder than a slab of Jenkins' barbeque ribs, the thin end." "So, you know the man the detective asked?" "He worked for me," the big man replied. "Your name sir," Biscuit asked the big man?

"My name, my name is Large Smalls and this is my son Bow, but people call him Extra." "Mr. Smalls, can you tell me the man's name?" "I don't know his given name. He walked up one day asking for work and I give him a job chopping and chunking wood. That been about a year ago now. We just call him Woodchopper." "Did he fill out an employment application or W-2 form?" asked Big Biscuit. "Ain't need nobody to fill out paper work. I needed a woodchopper and he was a damn good wood chopper." "Did he have friends or family?" "No, none I know of. To me he was a ghost down to the color of his skin," said Large Smalls, "He just showed up. He didn't say much and I didn't ask much. He was just Woodchopper." "Thank you, Mr. Smalls," the detective said. "We might need to ask you more questions before the investigation is over."

"But why Wood chopper," Large Smalls asked.

"He killed my friend and they needed someone to chop the timber to build his home in heaven," I replied as I turned and walked out the entrance.

"Don't just walk away from me," yelled Big Biscuit Bradley. "I want you down at the station in two hours for questioning."

Just then my cell phone rang. I pulled it from my front right pocket. It was 6:30am and Rosa was on the line. "Hey baby, you just waking up? It's been a long night but I'm on my way home. What's for breakfast? Leftover Jenkins' barbeque," Rosa told me. "No thanks, get ready we're going out to eat." After a quick stop at the apartment to shower and change clothes, Rosa and I rode over to the Cracker Barrel restaurant off JTB Boulevard. The morning fog had lifted and the sun was bright and new. I parked the truck and kissed Rosa on the lips before we exited and began walking across the parking lot. Rosa reached over and grabbed my left hand with her right then began to swing it as we walked. The cares of my early morning lifted and I felt as new as the sun rise, holding a rose that never wilts. I didn't just see the sun shining this morning, I saw the light. That light showed me that one day I would be back on the force. One day they'll call me back to do what I do. There's always going to be cold blooded monsters and someone has got to kill them. One day I'll make it all right again.

With a big smile on my face, Rosa and I went in and had breakfast. From our window seat, we enjoyed breakfast. We talked and smiled with the new sunrise shining on us. Until that is, the big black Mercedes rolled slowly through the parking lot, like a solar eclipse. From the window I could see it stop behind my truck. After several minutes it rolled to a position directly across from the window where Rosa and I sat. Not able to see inside for the dark black tinted windows. Knowing someone was getting a good long look. Still, I didn't want to alarm Rosa. Then the big black Mercedes drove off. I continued playing the lover outside while I had transformed to fighting mode inside. Shortly after we left the restaurant driving to downtown Jacksonville, it became clear to me how my life was being pulled down. Sure I had money from my investments but I had no status. I could hear detective Biscuit's words, 'you're not a cop anymore.' I needed status. Without it, I was swirling around in the drain of life slowly being sucked down. Running the streets seeking vengeance just made me a high level thug. Status was the life raft I desperately needed right now.

I reached my destination, The Jacksonville Police Memorial Building. I parked the truck and Rosa and I walked along Bay Street to the building. This was my home and these are my people. The black and white police cars parked along the street, uniform officers strolling, chatting and flashing their authority. Walking past just released inmates. You know they were just released by the big brown paper bag they're carrying with all their belongings and the wide eyed look of freedom on their faces. Cops shaking my hand, hugging me, and telling me how much they missed me. There wasn't enough time right now to tell them how much I missed them.

Reality hit me square in the face when I walked into the lobby. I had to sign in and have a seat with all the mothers, girlfriends, aunts and pimps waiting for someone to escort them in. Detective Jelly Belly Jackson came out and brought Rosa and I in. We took the elevator up to his office. Nothing smells like a police department with just waxed tile. Paper and ink from the copy machine and coffee. Along with the sound of hard sole shoes, keys giggling, paper shuffling and computer keys clicking. It was the smell and sound of status. Status I no longer had. After following Jelly Belly to his cubicle, Rosa began to look through a photo book to see if she could identify a suspect in her assault. I was then asked by the detective to accompany him to a private interview room where Big Biscuit was waiting. We all sat at a small table. "Hear me out, C.J.," Jelly said. "You know you're family here. In this department you get much love. I know you want to make a difference and do what's right by your friends and this city, but C.J. I can't be chasing killers and bandits and dealing with your mess!"

"You know getting the bad guy comes first to me detective, that's the job I do best".

"Yes, but you have to be working for somebody before you can be doing a job", said Jelly.

"What do you mean?" I asked. "I've got a job for you," Jelly told me.

"What?" I asked, "You can give me my badge back?" "No, no, it's not that," Biscuit said. "Then what, you want me to empty trash cans around the office?"

"Listen a minute," Jelly said. "I want to log you in as a C.I." "What? I responded, a confidential informant. You want me to go from being the best detective on the force to becoming a snitch?"

"No," Jelly Belly said. "C.J., I want you to go from rouge vigilante to working your way back to being the best detective on the force. Then, if there's any more trouble we're all covered."

At that moment, I remembered the bright new morning sunlight not just lighting up my day, but lighting up my way back. It wasn't much but for now it'll have to do. It was status. "I'll take it."

CHAPTER 15 – CHINA DOLL

I COMPLETED THE DETAILS of my new confidential informant status with the detectives. Now I got some status, this ain't just about me snitching bitches because when I find you I'm gonna blow you out your britches.

Back at detective Jelly Bellies' desk Rosa looks through the last line up book and still no face she can identify. "So what you got on Slick's murder?" I asked the detective. "I'm trying to track down gang leads right now. Part of the problem is everybody on the streets these days either looks like, acts like or associates themselves with gangs. Pants hanging, tattooed wearing, rap music blasting and that's the white kids in the suburbs. It's clouded the water so you can't tell the big fish from the crabs. They all carry knives, guns and if you stop their car they're subject to jump out blasting an AK-47 and that's just the girls."

"The last couple of months have been especially disturbing. We've had nearly two massacres a week, usually involving multiple victims, all known thugs with gang associations. Except for a few victims they all had been savagely cut and stabbed and left with five point stars or pentacles carved into their bodies. Like the massacre at the Putty Cat Lounge," he said. "Who you questioning," I asked.

"We've got no suspects at this time; no prints, no DNA, and nobodies seen O J. Oh, and one other thing. At least one body at each murder scene had some sort of tarot card folded and placed inside the mouth. Some real voodoo witchcraft shit."

"So you think this is all gang related?" "It could be, Jelly said, we're spreading through the streets checking chatter."

"On top of all that the Asian community and the mayor's office has a fire under my ass."

"The Asian community, you never hear anything from them. What's up with that?" I asked.

"They want those responsible for the rape and murder of the medical student that was volunteering free medical care to underprivileged kids at the Clanzel Brown Community Center. That's when all this bizarre shit started, she was the first and the only woman, Jelly said."

"I saw that in the news. She was Asian. I thought she was black." "She was mixed," said detective Biscuit. "She was black-Chinese. Her daddy is black and her mother is Chinese. She lived in China with her mother. She came to this country to complete her medical training and to be apart of the 'MTV-Hip hop save the world generation.' Many young people don't know there's a dark shadow behind the shiny bling. She was the first we found with the pentagram five pointed star carved into her chest and a tarot card of death folded and placed in her mouth."

"The Asian community has a huge financial stake in Jacksonville and they're pressing the mayor to get something done and he's putting a lot of pressure on this department to find who did it, Biscuit said."

"Is there anything associating her with gang action or thug life?" I asked him. "Nothing so far, she interned at the University Hospital in the emergency room. Worked part time for a health care temporary service agency and did volunteer work. She was a young woman who had dedicated her life to serving humanity", said Biscuit.

"Why weren't there any of these signs left on Slick's body, I asked the detectives."

"I don't know" Jelly said. "Maybe the killers were in a hurry, maybe they're different killers. Right now, we just don't know. Our closest lead so far is cooking in a pit on the south side."

"Which reminds me, it's past lunch time." "You guys hungry," Jelly asked Rosa and I.

"No thanks," we replied.

"Excuse me," he said before yelling to another officer across the room. "Hey Figaro, order up some Jenkins' barbeque for lunch, ribs with sauce on the side. We're burning the candle on both ends C.J. That's why I'm giving you a copy of my evidence file on this case. You track down leads, you contact me instead of burning them up." "I understand, but I do need something." "Anything but a badge," the detective responded. "The Albino said to me that someone was after my family. I need continuous security for Rosa and my kids." "I can do that, he said, but we don't have long to come up with something or the mayor's going to cut us all off and bring in some special task force."

"I would love nothing more than to bring justice to these victims and make the mayor happy, I responded to the detective.

As Rosa and I left the police station, I felt the case had gained a whole new mystery and intrigue. These new elements were leading down a new path for me. A path I've never ventured. It appears on the surface that there are people scheming in the dark not just to take down Jacksonville but an entire kingdom of light and truth. Like great conquerors of old, I believe I have God blessing my way to success.

I want to go and rest but I have to remember that jigga's in the street don't sleep, they grind night and day. God blesses even the birds but they still have to dig their own worms.

It will be a rough task getting to the bottom of all this, Slick's murder, the medical student's death, finding the African and the Dread. But if it ain't rough, it ain't right. I'm going to track them like a twister hunting for a trailer park. I would start with what appears to be the first clues. The medical student and what role tarot cards and pentacles play?

Rosa and I headed east out of downtown Jacksonville and over the Matthews Bridge. Then the Arlington Expressway took us to Barnes and Noble Book store. I'd need to do some research on these metaphysical symbols and hoped I might find a book or two. We entered the book store and it was like entering Neverland where dreams, visions, hopes and lives never die. They just morph into a book or a magazine. Everyone should spend more time in bookstores. There's a spirit about them that makes you feel smarter than you really are. There would definitely be less murder, robbery and assaults if we all spent more time in bookstores.

Rosa and I walked through the store and just before I started to ask for assistance. There it was, in the very back behind the religion section. I hoped they might have one or two books on the subject. There was a wall seven feet high and twelve feet long of books on ghosts, dreams, psychic powers, fallen angels, magic, spells, the occult, witches, fortune telling, tarot and astrology. This was a world I knew little of. I had never really explored. There's a scripture in the Holy Bible that says we fight not against flesh and blood but against powers, principalities and evil in high places.

I took three books from the shelves: 'Witches', 'The book of the Occult', and 'the Complete Idiot's guide to Tarot'. Rosa and I then walked over to the Café and grabbed a couple of cream caramel lattes. We got a table and I began to browse my books while Rosa went to the magazine rack and came back to the table with a Vogue, Glamour, and GQ magazine. The book 'Witches' spoke of the origins of witchcraft which today they refer to as the old religion. The book refers to witchcraft as a pagan religion of the earth and speaks of its churches reversing Christian symbols in order to redirect their power to the dark side. The pentacle is a prominent symbol used in satanic worship to defile God. Continuing on through books of the occult and the Tarot, they revealed to me that the death card symbolizes death as a higher status and consciousness raising experience.

All in all this is some disturbing shit. How do street thugs in Jacksonville get involved with witchcraft and occult symbols? Most of these brothers didn't get past ninth grade special education. I'm sure they didn't come to the bookstore and start studying up on it. Why the girl? The girl, it was then I realized I should know more about her, the girl.

I then pushed the books to the side and opened the evidence folder the detective gave to me. There, the top sheet, an 8 ½ by 11. A full color head shot. She was beautiful. Her hair was satiny black layers cut in a classic bob style with lash grazing bangs. The chic hair style framed a face that was perfectly molded porcelain, with teeth crafted of highest quality pearls and eyes that were perfectly round drops of black onyx. I slid the top copy and the next was a picture of the beautiful young woman with an older woman and young man about her age. It seems to be a family shot. They stood on a small bridge with a backdrop of lush green mountains and beautifully carved statues of oriental warriors. I slid the family photo aside to the third copy, the victim profile and there it was, her name: Natalie Parks, Height: 5'6" tall, 109 pounds. Occupation: Medical doctor, hometown: Shanghai, China. Any nicknames, yes she replied. What are they: China Doll. China Doll, no name has ever been so appropriate. No one has ever deserved less the brutal and cruel death she received. I slid the profile sheet aside to a photo of the crime scene. There she was, nude except her ankle strap high heels, laying face up on the three feet by three feet card table. Her arms and legs spread wide with her feet hanging from the table at the knees on one end and her head hanging off the other end of the table. There is blood smeared and dripping all over her body and a five star pentacle carved in the middle of her chest between her breasts.

I slid that photo to the side and the next is a close up of her face. Her satiny black hair is streaked with blood, her black onyx eyes are rolled back in the sockets. Her mouth is open and stuffed with a folded paper. I slid that sheet to the side and yet another picture. This, the unfolded, blood smeared card, the Tarot card of death. I paused and starred at the picture of the card for several minutes. Then, I staked the sheets back in the same order with her picture on top.

In my mind I spoke to her. Who? Who would do this to you China Doll? Whether it be witches, ghost, demons or Satan himself. I know the lives that me, Slick and these street hustlers live and the price we may have to pay. But you didn't deserve this, not you. Not you, Natalie Parks. Not you, China Doll.

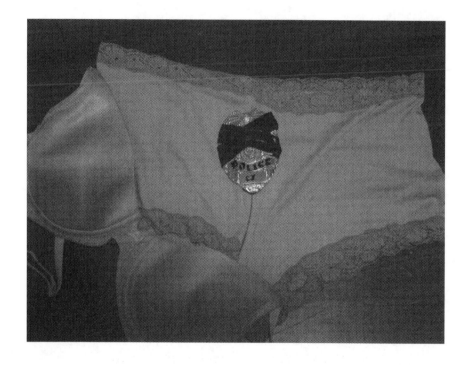

CHAPTER 16 – LOVE SHOWER

ROSA AND I finished our lattes at the book store and headed for the apartment. The ride was a quiet one even though Rosa tried to make conversation. I was not able just yet to release myself from the brutality China Doll had endured.

There's a trail these guys travel that led them to China Doll and beyond. If I pick up that trail it will lead me to them. This can end in one of two ways. They would not be caught then continue their rampage and hardly remember China Doll or I can catch them, bring them to justice and they never forget China Doll. I intend the latter.

Once we were back at the apartment hours without sleep and the bumps and bruises of my encounter with the Albino finally were catching up to me. A warm shower and late afternoon nap was just what I felt I needed. I went to the bathroom and undressed. Rosa put on a 'JAHEIM' CD and went into the kitchen to pour me a drink of Hennessy VSOP. I started my shower by standing under the warm stream of water and letting it sooth my fatigued body.

The shower curtain opened and there was Rosa completely nude. With her penthouse breast, playboy ass and heart shaped hustler pussy hair, handing me a shot of Hennessey. She was a hot little filly and I was bred to stud. One of the many things there are to appreciate about a good women is their ability to know what a man needs and what a man really needs.

I drank down the shot and handed her the glass which she placed in the sink. Then she stepped into the shower and turned me around so I was facing the shower head. Rosa reached over my shoulder and grabbed a tube of shower gel from the rack. She squeezed out a large portion over my back and shoulders. Then as the shower sprinkled the top of my head, she rubbed the lotion on my back and shoulder. Then slowly she stroked the lather down my butt and back of my thighs, then around to the front of my waist while pulling herself tight up against me. I could feel her nipples drawing passion sketches in my back. Both hands came up rubbing gel across each row of muscle in my stomach. She grabbed two hand fulls of my chest. On her tip toes she squeezed even tighter rubbing her pussy hair hard against my ass then started to slow grind me from the back.

Far behind now was the fatigue, long ago the pain, now only passion, passion sparking like lightening in a summer rain storm. I loosened her grip and turned around to her. Her long black hair wet from the shower and gel off my back. Her desire for me showed deep down in her dark Latino eyes. With my hands on her cheeks, I pulled her face close and began to kiss her hard and deep. She pulled herself close to me with her left arm and with her right hand positioned my erected dick between her thighs, here kitty kitty, then she reached up and rapped both arms around my neck. I grabbed her under the armpits and supported her as she stepped up on each side of the bath tub. She released my neck with her right hand and gripped the shower rod, as her body quivered she lowered herself onto my pussy primer. She's holding back a gusher, I can feel it. Every woman needs a dick that fits, and my dick fits her like the keys to a castle door. Rosa lifted her left leg off the edge of the tub and rapped it around my right thigh and squeezed hard, she knows how to get every drop of juice. Her tongue came out my mouth and she sucked up a deep breath like a pearl diver coming up for air. Her mouth moved to my right ear and whispered as though Delilah to Samson, give me all your strength. She lowered and straightened her right leg. Her rhythmic releasing and lifting of her body made for a smooth thrust of my dick into her pussy. I pushed long and hard like a drill into an oil well trying to hit a gusher. Her entire body was pulsating as she lifted and lowered herself onto my cock. I grabbed the back of her hair and licked her neck. She moaned like a little girl being disturbed from a good sleep. Then she double clutched her coochie and went to a higher gear.

The sweat, soap gel and shower spraying kept our bodies well lubricated. The frequency increased. Her deep breaths became short pants. She pushed and pulled her slit while my dick bell kept ringing her clit. Drool dripped from her bottom lip. Her grip slipped from the shower rod and she grabbed the top of the curtain. The thin plastic rings holding the shower curtain began to break and I could feel her weight shift and us loosing our balance. I bent my knees as the shower curtain came streaming down ring by ring. We slowly fell over, first on the edge of the tub then onto the tile floor with the curtain between us and the floor. Shower water splashing from the tub, the tip of my dick knocking on her nub. I move to a kneeling position to receive my pussy communion, Rosa sitting in my lap with both legs wrapped around my waist. My head down in her breast licking up her titties like the last bit of cake batter with dick all up in her stirring up pussy till I can't believe it's not butter.

The thrust got faster and the moans got louder. By now the plastic shower curtain was ripped into pieces. We slipped and slid all over the tile floor, with pussy splishing and water splashing, even without the shower I'd have her soaking wet.

I stood us up with me still wedged between her legs. It was clear to me she wasn't gonna take just nine, she wanted extra innings, hardball, curveball, sinker, she caught every pitch. My strike count was high but I won't pull myself out.

She lifted her left leg and propped her foot on the toilet lid. We bumped the sink until we knocked the soap and tooth brushes into the bowl. She reached back to get it and I turned her around and shot the pussy from the back with my cupid's arrow. She leaned over the sink and pressed the left side of her face against the mirror and was overcome by the fuck spirit as she then started to baby talk and moan "hit it, hit it." I went deep.

With her wet black strands of hair hanging across her eyes and mouth, Rosa's hands gripping the side of the sink, my hands gripping the two soft round pecan brown humps of her ass. With each pull and plunge we could hear items inside the medicine cabinet shake and fall. This was a fuck-a-thon and we were going to win, but the wet jiggling humps would slide free of my grasp each time we bumped the sink. Then with one movement she turned and grabbed my left hand and pulled me from the bathroom towards the bedroom. You could track us by the wet booty prints along the wall. Every two feet I was dropping the drill bit. When it seemed I was out, I kept cuming right back, I just knew I was close to the gusher.

We reached the bed where she laid me on my back and climbed on top. Rosa secured my dick up in her chastity then started humping me like a sixteen year old boy in the back seat of his daddy's station wagon on prom night. "What's my name? What's my name? Tell me my name bitch!"

"Rosa, Rosa, Rosa is your name", I answered her.

Her excitement grew and her pace quickened. My dick got harder than a frozen banana. Then the quiver, then the toes curl and the eyes roll back. Then the praise, Jesus! Jesus!" she exhaled. "Preach sister, preach," I responded. Then her body went limp.

"C.J. baby, thank you. I guess I should go turn off the shower," Rosa said. I then rolled on top. "You're not done yet?" She asked. "You know I'm not done till the sweat drips through the box springs."

Rosa then slid her arms under mine and gripped my shoulder blades deep with her manicured nails, then kissed my neck, squeezed her thighs and gave me a reason to always hurry home. I started to give her that really good dick. The bed rocking, pussy popping, room shaking like a Tokyo earthquake, head whip lashing from the mattress recoil. All the nuts and jolts loosen the bed's nuts and bolts.

We bumper car half our bodies off the bed, Rosa's head became lodged between the mattress and the night stand, but I kept hitting that tail till it jack in the boxed up.

Just in time. That pussy started oozing love like a cracked honey comb. "Sus et salir a chorros", she yelled in Spanish. "Yeah, baby, it's a gusher alright. It's a gusher."

INTERMISSION: Take this time to fuck your mate. I'll wait

CHAPTER 17 – HOME

I woke early the next morning to what I thought was the sound of rain. It was only the shower we had not cut off from the night before. Needless to say there was no hot water left, probably in the whole block. I put on a pot of coffee and pulled out the evidence folder. It's hard to sleep when you're in the game this deep. Somewhere in the pictures, the statements and the profiles there had to be some clues. Of all the women in this town, why China Doll? What is the connection between China Doll, Slick and these thugs being murdered around town?

I stood at the kitchen counter watching the coffee brew. Thinking what might have been different had I not been late for my meeting with Slick. It was about 5:00am when I went back into the bedroom for my bathrobe and sandals trying not to disturb Rosa sleeping soundly in the dry spot. I walked out of the apartment with my cup of coffee to sit and think on the front steps.

I walked out in time to see the big black Mercedes with the black tinted windows. It was identical to the one that prowled the parking lot at the Cracker Barrel restaurant. Just as I saw it, it sped past the young officer asleep in his patrol car. The officer assigned to protect Rosa. The Spirit is willing but the flesh is weak. With the Mercedes out of sight I cautiously sat observing an owl in a nearby tree and several dolphins leaping from the moonlit river water across the street. I could hear the river water splashing against the concrete barrier and the future speaking to me that the answers were in the past. I must go back if I want to discover what's ahead of me. I decided to go back home.

The place I was raised and left a hero. The place Slick never left; home, where they boast of me being a big time city cop, my home, where I was an example to young brothers as a responsible family man. Back when I had a wife, family and rocketing career. Before my divorce and before the car crashed and my career was wrecked. Knowing I'd have to pretend everything was fine and that Slick was dead. I've got to go back home, but first I walked to the curve and woke the patrolman assigned to watch Rosa.

I dressed and had breakfast with Rosa before I left the San Marco apartment heading southwest to Orange Park, Florida. My family has history in Orange Park. It had a history of hard working parents and grandparents. Shotgun shacks, out houses and wood burning stoves. They were folks that worked turpentine fields, farms and any work white folks would give out. Over time they raised some educated children who used their learning to go from the farm to the faculty staff. Their children rose from planters and pickers to pulpits and practitioners, a religious people who spent all day Sunday at church trying to get Jesus on the main line.

My thirty minute drive had brought me to the center of Orange Park traveling east on Kingsley Avenue. I reached the road just before the railroad tracks. Of course it's Railroad Avenue and of course black folks live there. My folks live there. Before stopping at my parent's home I decided to take a drive through the community. You can revisit memories here because even though the world is changing fast, things change slowly in the hood. A right onto McDower Lane and three houses on the left Uncle George is sitting on his front porch. I stopped my truck in the middle of the road then run up the walkway to hug him. "I can't stop, but I'll be back," I tell him. "We'll go fishing," I yell as I pull off. I was home. I could feel it all down in my soul. I drove down to the park where Slick and I played baseball and football.

God bless all those people who commit their time building young lives. Then another left at Filmore Street where the locals are holding social hour under the big oak tree, they're playing cards and checkers, talking sports, politics, religion and sex. You want to know how to change a carburetor or cook a possum, this is the spot. I slow down and wave as I go by, then back on Railroad Ave just a few blocks from my parent's, I've got one more stop.

Ms. Quinetta's the best cook in town. You could open a four star restaurant selling her left over meats, poultry, fish, potatoes, rice, salads, cakes, cookies and sorbets. Foods so delicious it'll make you nut in your good underwear. I swear to God!

I pulled my truck over in front of her house, around the other eight cars parked out front. I'm not the only one who knows about Ms. Quinetta's cooking. I ran up and rang the doorbell and this beautiful fortyish black Julia Child opens the door. With a big beautiful smile she says, "Hey, C.J.! Come here, boy. Give me a hug." I can smell something cooking as she grabs me and gives me a big kiss on the cheek. Not only could I smell the food, I could see all the people already sitting around her table. Eleven a.m. and the house is full. At one end is Mr. Julius, the school principal and at the other is retired police chief, Mr. Joe. Then there's Dennis the contractor, Carlos the musician, Ms. Felicia the postal Clerk, Ms. Juliet the computer tech, Ms. Karen the insurance agent and Ms. May the housewife. Just when I thought I had counted all the stomachs the church deacon came from the back. She operates a Godly home and provides for friends, widows, orphans and the elderly. "I just wanted to stop by to say hello Ms. Quinetta, since I was passing by."

"Stop playing, boy," she told me, I know why you came by. Sit down let me fix you a plate." I sat and watched and listened to all the love and laughter in the room brought about by the delicious meal Ms. Quinetta had prepared. I joined in and after seven or eight minutes, Ms. Quinetta had bagged up plates of fish and shrimp and roasted chicken completed with all the sides. For dessert, she gave me a plate piled with homemade chocolate cake and cookies. "Thank you, Ms. Quinetta." "You welcome, boy. How's you mamma doing?" "She's good. I'm on my way to see her now," I said. "Tell her I said hello and you stay longer next time." "Yes, ma'am, I will." I hugged her and went to my truck with a big smile on my face then drove the next couple of blocks engulfed in an aromatic fog of culinary genius.

I've reached my parent's home and I can't wait to sit with my plates and a bottle of hot sauce and get stupid full. No fat gram or cholesterol counting today. I'm going to eat in honor of all the obese people everywhere. I rang the doorbell; my father answered the door wearing a short sleeved plaid shirt and paisley print boxer shorts. "C.J.! What's up, my boy?"

"Hello, pop."

"What you got there boy"

"It's a few plates I picked up from Ms. Quinetta's." Before I could get the last syllable of Ms. Quinetta's name out, pop grabbed the bags from my hand. "You know that girl sure can cook, but don't tell you mama I said that. She's in the bedroom. I know she'll be glad to see you." I stood paralyzed as my father, like the head lion, carried away my fresh kill. From his recliner he roared, "Hand me a fork and some hot sauce from the kitchen. Thanks for looking out for your daddy C.J."

I could only watch as he ripped meat from bone. "C.J., is that you Honey, that you in there?"

My mother's calling from the bedroom. "Yes, ma, it's me." "Well, come on back." My mother is perched on the side of her bed wearing a pink Capri pants suite, her gray hair in tight rolls. With a phone book open on her lap. I kiss her on the cheek and ask what she's doing. "I'm a woman on the go. Can't you tell? I have to be, because your daddy sure ain't going to get out that chair and do nothing."

I sat next to her on the bed. "Honey, I'm so glad you're home."

"Thank you ma, it's good to be home!"

CHAPTER 18 – KANDI STOWE

TIME SPENT AND respects paid, now it's time to go back to work for my friend who was slain!

I walked out of my parent's door and across the street to Slick's parent's home. I knock on the door. His mother answers. "I expected to see you before now," she said to me. I had no response. She began to cry, and then I stepped inside the doorway and put my arms around her. "Why did this happen, C.J.? Why?" It had been days now sense I felt the full weight of Slick's death on my soul. "What went wrong in his life? Lord, knows I did all I could to raise my children."

"Yes, ma'am, you did your best." "I won't stop until I have the answers for you, I told her."

"You know Slick really looked up to you C.J." "I know he was the friend God sent to me and I want to know why he's gone too."

"The neighborhood used to be full of joy and music. Now it seems as though there's nothing but death in the air, she said. C.J., me and my husband live for the Lord, now. So forgive me for this, but if I ever see the people that did this, I want to see them lined in chalk. I want it like a chicken wants corn. You understand where I'm coming from?" She asked. "Trust me, I'm on my grind and there will be no rest for the wicked, I told her."

"Well, then you go see that Jezebel over off 103rd Street he was seeing and take extra bullets." I looked into her eyes and could see the commission I was being charged to carry out. I could feel the eagle spirit within me soaring before I could get out the door. I responded with a smile to comfort her and told her I wouldn't let her down. Back in my truck headed west like a hard riding sheriff going after the outlaw. Judgment is coming. Judgment is coming.

There was a time when trouble on the Westside had to do with drunken rednecks fighting with their spouses. Flea Markets, rebel flag, southern comfort and country music, it was a regular peckerwood paradise. That was before government assisted low income apartment complexes became the new projects. Single black mothers came with their children. Their baby's daddies soon followed. The baby's daddies brought the hustles and staked out the territory.

In India they say rats bring rat snakes and rat snakes bring king cobras. Drunken brawls became gunfights. Killings bring retaliation. The threat of killings and retaliation bring terror to the community. Fear and loathing spread like crabgrass and chinch bugs. Learning, growth, joy and pride are stunted.

What you're left with is Urica Plantation Apartments off interstate 295 and 103rd street on Jacksonville's Westside. The Urica Plantation is patrolled by young black Alqueda known as the Urica Plantation Goons. This is a flea market of gambling, drugs, bootleg liquor and food stamp fraud. It's a harsh game. But there are children being raised in this hopeless haze and that's real.

Many are the descendants of African kings and queens. Stuck with mother's who never learned more than to duck and fuck. Children are sent to school at five or six not knowing how to count pass five or six. Teenagers don't stand a chance if they're never taught nothing but to sling rock and dance. No parents to raise them, no food to eat, no education, no clothes that fit, hell maybe the starving kids in Africa will hold a telethon for them. It's not all violence and intimidation that keeps people in places like Urica Plantation. The high speed, adrenalin rushing, juiced up life of sex, drugs, hustling and drama can hook you in deep.

The four rows of three story apartment buildings form a square with a large open courtyard in the center. I parked my truck near the corner. As I walk up, I could see blinds crack and curtains pull back with eyes peaking through. The word was out, a stranger approached, rooftop lookouts as young as nine and ten sounding the alarm.

Young teenage girls wearing flirt skirts with three inch heels and push up bras flash their best Victoria secret pose while pulling along little four and five year olds. Young brothers with hard looks, pants hanging, stand in doorways mumbling rap lyrics.

Many of the apartment numbers had been scratched off but not hers. I made my way across the dirt courtyard to apartment number 187 and knocked on the door. The door opened slowly as if the person inside still wanted to give you time to walk away.

Then she appeared, five feet seven, 34-20-38, about 150 pounds. Kandi Stowe, Urica Plantation's queen bee. She's got on a red Lenin baby doll halter dress with a v-neck and standing tall in a pair of two inch slide sandals. Her hair is red and black strands up in big Shirley Temple curls. Kandi's smoking a thin cigar. I wait for her to speak first. She steps up closer then exhales a long slow drag of smoke. I hear old school R&B music playing in the background. Without saying a word, she turns and walks back into the apartment.

I followed her the short distance to the living room with its black leather sofa and loveseat. A young girl, about eight years old lies on the floor watching television. I sat on the sofa. Kandi sat on the arm rest.

"What happened to Slick?" I asked.

"He got killed."

"I know he was killed! Who did it and why?"

"Hey, Katie," she said to the child watching television. "Yes, ma'am," "Get a glass of kool aid from the refrigerator and go watch TV in my room and close the door," "Yes, ma'am." The child answered then carried out the instructions.

"That's all you really want?" Kandi asked.

"What do you mean?" I said. "Cause jiggaz come up here wanting other things: weed, coke, ass…

"I want you to tell me about Slick!"

"What's to tell? He could fuck and he could pay." "That's all you can say!" Slick's dead and that's all you can say?" "He lived longer than most jiggaz around here, Kandi responded.

"Did anybody come by to see him?" "A dude came by in a big black Mercedes with black tinted windows. He never got out and I never saw him. Slick would get in, he said he was about to make some big money."

"Did Slick ever say the dude's name?" Kandi then lifted a card from the sofa end table and handed it to me. "This is the card he gave Slick." It was a tarot card. "What does it mean?" I asked. "I don't know, Kandi said, but there's a phone number on the back." "Did you dial the number?" I asked Kandi. "I did and got some physic wanting to make me an appointment for a reading." I put the card in my pocket.

"Thanks Kandi, for your help. You need a couple bucks?" Kandi then stood and faced me. "Slick's gone and he ain't coming back, she said; what I need from you goes deeper than a roll of dimes."

"What's Kandi got to do to get a stimulus package," she asked as her arms slipped through the straps holding the red halter dress. The dress slid down over the curves of her African goddess form like a towel sliding off a just waxed sports car. Pass the nipples, down the waist and over the smooth round ass, flashing that fatty. No panties!

"The Stowe is open. Let Kandi satisfy your sweet tooth." "That's nice Kandi but I have a charge to keep and a calling to avenge my friend."

"So you're not going to fuck me!" Kandi said. With all my strength I fought back my lust for female flesh with the word, "no!"

"I ain't gonna charge you, right now Kandi's sugar free, I'd be good for you even if you were diabetic. Zip down your pants lets share a tootsie roll."

"Sorry Kandi I've got to find this rotten meat before I can eat, destiny is calling me."

"Yeah but I just want to wet your whistle before you go."

"No!"

Kandi straddled her big thighs over the arm rest. "Don't leave Kandi with all this sugar," she said. Kandi then started squeezing the sofa fabric between her legs so tight and hunching so hard she was rubbing the pleather off the fabric.

Her pubic hairs were sparking up like a summer brush fire, all the while pleading, "fuck me! fuck me! I ain't been fucked all day!"

My mouth watered and my tooth ached, then I swallowed a big gulp of my own spit. I pulled myself up off the sofa and began to back out the room.

Kandi kept riding that arm rest like a bar room bronking bull.

"Till we meet again, till we meet again, Kandi Stowe"

CHAPTER 19 – BEHOLD THE BLACK HORSE

AS I LEFT Kandi's apartment with the picture of her naked body and big curly hair saddled over the sofa's arm rest still in my eyes, I felt I had dodged a bullet that would keep me from accomplishing my mission.

Walking across the dirt courtyard, I noticed there were no more peering eyes from windows and blinds. Nobody standing in doorways watching, I may not have dodged my last bullet yet.

Suddenly I was alone. Something wasn't right. I could feel my senses heighten. The rats and rabbits don't run and hide unless there's a hawk approaching.

I made my way to the corridor exiting the complex. As I exit, I could hear the rubber squeal as car tires were braking. I saw two cars come to a halt near the entrance to the gate that surrounds the complex. Two men exit the first vehicle, one from the rear driver's side and the other from the front passenger's side, two of the Urica Plantation Goons carrying large caliber pistols.

I knew because I saw the guns and they were wearing t-shirts that read Urica Plantation Goons. I started a full sprint to the gate entrance which was about 20 yards away. The two goons raised their guns and began to fire. I was at top speed when I exited the gate, with bullets matrixing all around me, then dove head first over the hood of the old silver ford Taurus.

At the same time reaching for the double holstered 45's strapped to my back under the oversized black Sean John shirt and jeans. I tumbled and rolled head first over the hood then on the pavement. I came up gripping the forty five's. From a crouch and pivot position, I began blasting my double dirty Harries. Within a ten yard red zone, we were setting it off. One goon in the street got two in the chest; the one on the sidewalk took one to the shoulder then one through the bicep. He couldn't lift his pistol after the bullet tore through muscle and tendons, but he kept firing, shooting himself in both feet, then he fell to the ground screaming like a bitch.

The driver of the first vehicle began firing an automatic weapon through the windshield. I ducked and shuttled from one side of the ford Taurus to the other. He stopped, I think to reload. When I looked up three men got out of the second car. Two from the front and Vernon who had said he would hold me responsible if anything happened to his brother at the strip club from the rear passenger side. He doesn't know I had nothing to do with his brother, George's death. Now's not the time to try and explain it to him. Vernon was carrying a Russian style AK-47 riffle in his right hand and several replacement banana clips in his left hand. The two goons posted up behind parked cars on both sides of the street. Vernon started to take aim. This whole block was about to get hot. I dare not turn my back and try to run the thirty yards to the corner.

But right then an unexpected moment of saving grace. Vernon and the goons paused for a car coming up behind them. As the little compact car passed them and approached me, I lounged towards it hooking my left arm on the driver side mirror. Vernon and the goons opened up. The driver sped up and I quickly made the distance to my truck. I pulled my keys, popped the lock and jumped in.

All hell was breaking loose. The two goons on the side of the street were firing big banging hand guns while Vernon and the driver of the first vehicle fired automatic weapons. All the while magnum shells are sprinkling the pavement and dance to the sound of booming steel and tinkling brass. The air was full of pierced metal, shattered glass and mussel smoke. I cranked up the truck then turned in the cab and straddled the center console. I began firing through what was left of the rear window. With both guns empty I turned back into the driver's seat and peeled out.

Damn you, Vernon! I was going to ask you for an edge but you're trying to part my skull!

I got away! I could call Biscuit and Jelly and plan some type of take down against Vernon and the goons. But I'd just waste time. They would bring in detectives to talk to witnesses and gather statements. There'd be no one who heard or would say anything. It's the code. The code they live by in the hood. Hear no evil, see no evil, you snitch you die.

Anyway, I had what I needed, the tarot card, the phone number and again the mysterious black Mercedes. Before I could make more moves and track more clues I needed a new ride. My truck had served me well, but now riddled with bullet holes and most of the glass shot out, I needed to park it and switch up. I hit the interstate then exited onto Commercial Boulevard.

I pulled up to Tower Auto Detailing, a business venture I backed several years ago that's paid off quite well. I store a vehicle in one of their rear units. I park the truck and unlock the units steel roll up door. You can almost hear it stirring from its sleep. The gate rolls up and there it is under the imported black Italian micro fiber cover. I got it at a federal auction about a year ago seized in a drug bust. I yanked once on the cover and it dropped to the floor like an unstrapped silk teddy. Like Marilyn Monroe's skirt blowing up and revealing her goodies. There, jet black with black interior, Pirelli racing tires rapped around chrome and black Gianni rims. The only thing missing was a half naked super model in stiletto heels standing next to it.

It's my Ferrari 360 Modena. She's a bad bitch with a whole lot of horsepower. Keeps her wet, keep's him hard and I look damn good in it. I slid my ass down in her like it was the first time then pushed slowly up and down on her throttle to get her fluid going. I clicked her key, first she purred. I pressed harder, and then she roared. I pumped her a couple of times and she screamed. She was ready. I pulled out then tipped Art, my Detail Man, and rode off the property, the stallion on the black horse carrying the long sword, gleaming and stunt'n harder than Braveheart.

I return to the apartment where I give a wave to the patrolman assigned to protect Rosa. Inside, I listen to Rosa tell me about her day, a day without incident. I don't want to alarm her with my bullshit and drama. While Rosa prepared dinner I dialed the number on the tarot car, 843-3323.

A woman answered, "Hello, Madam Discovery," she said, "I give past, present and future readings. Would you like to set up and appointment? Yes, I would," I answer. "What time can I see you tomorrow?" "Is three o'clock, o.k.?" Yes, sir. That will be 35 for past 45 for present and 60 for future, your name please? I'm C.J. Thank you, Mr. C.J. Ms. Discovery will see you at 3:00pm tomorrow."

I listened and laughed with Rosa till time for bed. With my doo-rag on my head, my pistol on my right and my pussy on my left, I fell asleep.

CHAPTER 20 – BADD BOYZ BARBER SHOP

THE SKY WAS so blue. The grass is so green. The bright orange sun was the only thing bigger than the smiles on the faces of the people holding hands and singing. Beautiful people, the most beautiful people I've ever seen. Not just physically, but that they had a truth and purity and innocence that people don't have where I'm from. We walked and skipped and sang until they let my hand go and began to skip away.

I kept reaching out but they continued moving farther away. I could see them looking beyond me. Someone's calling you. Someone's calling you they said as I tried to catch up and regain my spot. I looked back and could see the valley with heat rising from its dry hot sand and rocks, scattered with bones of dead people. It's the valley of death. With a woman's voice echoing from the valley. C.J.! C.J.!

A closer look at the bones and I could see their faces had shape. In the face of the bones, I could see Slick, China Doll and all the victims I've seen over my years as a cop. Then, the ground and the rocks started to shake and the beautiful people were moving farther and farther away and the voice from the valley got louder. C.J.! C.J.! The bones then rose up out of the dry hot sand and began to walk towards me. All calling my name as the ground shook. "What? What is it?" I asked as they moved closer and encircled me. Seek the dead, they said, seek the dead, seek the dead. The bones repeated over and over again. "What does that mean? seek the dead? I'm not dead. What does that mean?" The bones shouted again, seek the dead jigga! Seek the dead you motherfucking jigga!

That scene faded from vision and there was Rosa standing next to the bed shaking me awake. "C.J., your phone is ringing. That must have been some dream you were having," she said as she turned and walked to the living room. I told her I heard someone calling my name, it's hard to sleep when you're deep in the game. Then I grabbed the ringing cell phone with my right hand and pushed receive. It was detective Biscuit. C.J.! "Yeah, what's up?" "C.J., you had beef with Vernon", he asked? Vernon and his goons got beef with me, but I'll have to deal with that later. I got too much on my plate right now." "Well, now is later, get down to Badd Boyz Barber Shop. Your plate just got fuller." I slammed the phone down. Back to reality!

I didn't need a physic to tell me what I was in store for as I got out of the bed a different person than the one who laid down the night before. Dream or no dream, I had to leave my friend and China Doll and the other innocent victims in the hot sand and rock of the valley of death. They didn't deserve to be there. Somebody does deserve to be there, the African and Black Dread and I'm going to find them and send them. Welcome C.J., welcome to the Club of Jacksonville's most vile, cruel, unremorseful, unrepentant, and disrespectful. Welcome to Jigga!

I walked to the closet and pulled the sliding doors. I stand there staring into the rows of clothing, hate and vendetta oozing from my pores like juice from a jeri curl, coming from places deep inside of me, generations deep. From the jiggaz who high-jacked royalty and sold it to European's who traded that royalty in the slave markets of America. To the jiggaz carjacking the descendents of royalty today and leaving them dead on the side of dirt pits. What the fuck you expect from a jigga! A Street corner killing for a fake Rolex, a home invasion for a flat screen TV. It aint racial profiling if the jigga did it! A senseless killing of a beautiful young medical intern, tattoo's on your neck, don't you know you'll never make a decent paycheck, jigga! What the fuck else do you want from a jigga? He could grow into a man if his mama stops babying him. No school clothes and no pens or paper bought, but it's not his fault, he spent the money on a case of Schlitz malt, jigga!

There has been and will continue to be an element of society that will relish in being Jiggaz. Regardless of race or creed they rebel in their deviant life style. Capri pant wearing, pimp walking, shit talking, always on the corner stalking, jigga! Robbing, assaulting and killing. Refuse to pull up your pants and edge up them dreads even if it means moving from Special Ed to getting ahead, Jigga! Killing people like China Doll and Slick. Live with your mama, grandmamma and welfare baby mama, Jigga! Would rather do a bid than work minimum wage and take care of your kid! Tittie sucking jigga! Cursing in public and shaming your people, of course nobody said anything, who can talk to your dumb ass. Break in my house and steal my silverware but you don't even eat with a spoon or a fork, God damn jigga! Teenage jiggaz robbing, murdering and raping, where's a black preacher protest when you need one. You dropped out of kindergarten, dropped out of grade school, dropped out of high school, now you say you got to rob people because no one will give you a good job. Doing what? Go back to school you stupid motherfucking jigga!

Line this hymn, eight to eighty, blind, cripple or crazy if you take a life we're going to fill your ass with electricity till you ain't got a life. Die in hell souless jigga! Kill a fifty-seven year old white woman out delivering pizza. You ain't got but one defense, read Leviticus 9 before I hit you in the face with these hollow point nines, you black hearted jigga! You two jiggaz killed that girl from U C now you got to D I E. Tell Satan C.J. sent you. To the cold blooded, piece of shit jigga that murdered the Haitian maintenance man at the Baymeadows Mcdonald's, we're going to pump you with no-doze while every part of your body is amputated. Then drink gasoline and piss on your body parts then set them on fire. He could survive an earth quake, but no one can survive an ignorant ass motherfucking jigga! Fuck that prison rehabilitation shit, the only job for you is working the chain gang in Iraq digging up IED's. It's so wack, all these jiggaz running round killing blacks. Black women cut us some slack, if that baby comes out evil hit it with an axe. If you don't it will grow up, kill you, cut your head off and put it in a sack. Then go to church and teach the new members class while the congregation chants Omen.

So many innocent lives bounced and all you get is life and a day, just ask Islam that ain't the way. You balance the check with a sword to the neck it's the only way for a jigga to pay. Born again my ass, jiggaz took lives and nobody told, you'll spend eternity in a fiery black hole. Pay your tithes, usher, sing in the choir and take communion, you're still going to hell, Satan's holding a family reunion. Jigga for life.

I knew why I woke with this hate leaking from my soul. Why something had woken the dark part of myself. It was the answer to the question. How do you bring a jigga to his knees? How do you stop a jigga? How do you kill a jigga? What is his natural predator? Another jigga!

I was the answer to the question. I had to be a jigga to stop a jigga! That's when I opened the steel pistol box on the top shelf of the closet. I took out the Smith and Wesson short nose 22 special and the black 44 magnum with the blue titanium steal cylinders. I got that knew ammo to pierce those Kevlar vest so three in the chest, two in the neck will get that jigga good and wet. Sure his mama gone cry but you aim and pull the tripper and tell a jigga bye-bye. I can't forget my black stainless steel Gucci watch. If a jigga is going killing he should be matching. I also pulled a black t-shirt, a pair of black Gucci jeans with black Jeff Banks flat nose string up leather shoes and my black waist length Hugo Boss leather jacket.

I walked out of the apartment feeling like the bright morning sunlight was a spot light just on me. Holding my nuts and smoking a black and mild, I gave a 'thumbs up' to the patrolman stationed out front. I step in and fired up the Ferrari, tilted the rear view mirror towards my face. I looked into the eyes in the mirror. I was treading knee deep in hate and furry. To that man in the mirror, I had just one thing to say, Ride, you mother fucking jigga, ride. I smashed the accelerator to the floor and fish-tailed out of the parking space and around the corner with the Ferrari screaming for mercy. With the speed of the Greek God Mercury and the passion of Christ, I claimed the fast lane of San Jose Boulevard. The accelerator pressed deep into the guts of the 360 Medina. I covered the thirteen or so miles to Badd Boyz Barber Shop in mere minutes. I pulled up to the scene with rescue units, cop cars, ambulances, coroner vans and lots of crime scene tape, then parked my car on the grassy area just off the side street across from the little strip mall. I approached the front of the shop with its black painted glass located between the ice cream shop and the pizza parlor.

The door to Badd Boyz opened and I was standing face to face with Detective Jelly. "When did you last see Vernon", he asked? "Yesterday afternoon. He and some of his goons tried to jump me. We shot it out and

I got away. I was going to report it hoping you might pick them up later". "We're picking his goons up now, we just need to know which pieces go with which." The detective moved aside to allow me entrance to the shop. This was another vicious, senseless, unconscionable slaughter. Slavery and hundreds of years of racism ain't got nothing on the evil that one jigga can bring to another these days. The bodies of what seems to be four men were sprawled around the room. The bodies had been cut, slashed and amputated, with a five pointed star carved in each forehead and a folded tarot card stuck in the mouth.

Vernon sat in the first barber's chair to the right looking dazed, covered in blood, holding two handguns but still alive. Another guy's head bobbed in the big fish tank near the front window. Maybe those were his body parts on the pool table in the back of the room. Severed arms, legs and heads thrown around the room make three more bodies. Blood and guts splashed across chairs, mirrors and walls. There on the rear wall just as with the Putty Cat strip club. Written in blood, 'Never the righteous forsaken'. I step to the front of the barber's chair then lean over and ask, "Vernon what happen?"

"The lights went out he said, then he came through the back, all I saw was a lean athletic figure in black. Sword swinging with a sound like it was slicing through wind, cutting off parts of jiggaz again and again. First to fall was that big fat jigga C-Force, he cut his arm, leg, then his head. Then Muscle Mike, he tried to run but got hit in his back, the sword severed both his legs then his head. He cut his way through the rest of them, then I blasted the room with both these berettas, he ducked and dodged the bullets like I was just throwing feathers. He had slashed up the room, all but me, as he approached with his sword in one hand and a big knife in the other I laid out my plea. In my family they all depend on me, you've already killed my brother, what will they tell my mother? I fell back into my barber's chair waiting to receive my cut. His sword raised, his knife pulled back, then time slowed and I remembered from days back. I'd see my old pastor and he'd tell me it's still time to come back. But as I looked into the fiery eyes of the dark villain I felt that train might have left me. Still as a last resort I called out Jesus, just in case my mamma's prayers may have kept me. Jesus! Jesus! I shouted, at that moment when my bullets and my guns could not save me and I sat facing my sins and all the wrong things I did.

A bright light pierced through the dark painted store front glass blinding the villain and halting his attack. A bright light, saving grace, a revelation that I could be saved and in turn save others that cross my path. I could do a lot of good with Badd Boyz barber shop."

Vernon had been saved, the light of God's love had forced out the dark villain, but where was he? Who was he?

This was something deep in the heart of the perpetrator. This was personal, real personal. Someone has brought a new level of evil to town, thugs and hustlers being knifed up. Slick and China Doll and God knows who else. I don't have a clue yet what this is all about. Is it a lust for blood, a fight for territory or someone's idea of sick fucking fun? Why would the African or Black dread kill Vernon's goons or did they? Has someone else done all this killing? I've got to solve this riddle and catch these jokers.

"Do you have any other witnesses? Did anybody else see anything?" I asked Biscuit and Jelly.

"There's the bus driver," responded Jelly.

"What about the bus driver?" I asked.

"The route driver from midnight till 8:00am said there was a guy sitting at the bus stop from 2:00am 'til day break. The bus would stop each pass but the guy never got on. He's next door in the pizza parlor."

The Detectives and I headed for the pizza parlor leaving Vernon and a trail of bloody shoe prints with each step. Inside, near the front window sat a neatly groomed black man in a bus driver's uniform. He stands, and then shakes my hand. "Thank you for waiting, sir. I'm C.J. What can you tell us about the man at the bus stop?" "He wore all black. He looked lean and strong. There was something foreign about his face and eyes. Eyes that stared as if they had seen terrible things, things that burn inside of a man, maybe things like what happened next door." "Thank you for your time," Detective Biscuit said, "We'd like to ride you downtown to have a sketch artist assist you with a picture of the suspect." I turned and walked to the door.

"Where are you going?" asked Detective Biscuit. "I'm sick of arriving at the crime scenes after the fact. I'm going to find out the future." Detective Jelly laughed. "It sounds like you're going to see a fortune teller." "I am," I answered, then pushed open the door of the pizzeria and left.

CHAPTER 21 – MS. MIRIAM

WALKING THROUGH THE on-lookers and across the street to my car like a trained bloodhound there two scents I can track day or night. That's spilt blood and pussy.

Whoever has committed this crime has blood on them. I fire up the Ferrari and kick up dirt as I spin out in the grass then burn rubber on the black top. I'm early for my appointment but any information Madame Discovery might have I need right now. As I set new speed limits from light to light. I can't help but think of Vernon with his goons all cut up like that.

Black men's lives are being snatched up like the rapture. Everyday there's enough jigga's in the obituaries to make a Tarzan movie. If black people invested into General Motors what they invest in obituaries, every black person in this country would be driving a new Cadillac.

I hit the gas on my 500 horse power black surf board and rode the paved wave down Beach Boulevard to Madame Discovery's. I arrive at the iron gated compound and turn onto the acre property then drive the dirt drive way past the old faded, broken, half hanging sign that read 'Madame Discovery, Psychic.' I stopped my car a few yards from the wooden house. In a blink everything seemed wrong. The bright sunny day was gone. Darkness and fog engulfed the property. Amidst a moonlit glow appeared black birds and crows on the ground, the house and my car. I started to get out. Then he appeared out of the dark fog, a giant of a brother, twice the size of a regular man. He must have been seven foot fourteen and five hundred pounds. His pants and shirt barely reached his calves and forearms. He was barefooted and had a big Frankenstein type ball head. He used one of his fish net sized hands to open my door. Then bent over and says to me, "Ms. Discovery don't like nobody parking on the grass." But there wasn't no grass; the entire property was sandy dirt. "My name is Pastor Darryl," he says "Nice to meet you, Pastor Darryl". "You can go right in," Pastor Darryl said as he pointed to the screen door of the old house. He then turned and walked back into the fog while making hand gestures and talking to himself.

As I approach the wooden railing and red brick steps leading up to the small porch, I see two rather large figures to my right. The fog lightens and standing next to the railing are two large great Danes, the horse of all dogs. They scared the piss out of me. I could feel a little drip down my left leg. One of the large dogs is solid black with grayish eyes and the other black and white with eyes like cat eye marbles. Both stared but never growled or charged. "Come, come. I've been waiting for you," the voice inside the screen door said. I pulled myself up the wooden railing to the small porch. When I reached the screen door the two dogs had moved to the bottom of the stairs. I opened the screen door and stepped into an emporium of years past. There were glass cases with shelves holding canisters of cookies, candies, and bubble gum, a soft drink cooler next to a pinball machine on my left then to my right a juke box. Above the Juke Box is a painting. My eyes focus on the painting as I move closer. It's got my attention because it's a painting of the old house with the two great Danes out front next to a black Ferrari and a dude who is dressed and looks a lot like me. I was moving in for a closer look when again the voice called, "Come in." The voice was coming from a dark hallway leading to another room in the house. I stepped into the hallway, it was black, like I imagined the inside of a coffin would be. I took a few steps then turned my head to look back and it was only pitch black behind me. Carefully, I placed one foot in front of the other and moved forward.

Suddenly, above my head there were stars. I find myself standing in a barely lit room with a small table on which sat a glass ball. I leaned over to look closer at the glass ball when from behind me the voice asked, "Why you called the dead?" I quickly spun around. "What the fuck? You scared the shit out of me," I said to the little dark haired, dark eyed women dressed in black standing behind me. Again she asked, "Why you call the dead?"

"Madame Discovery, you need to break that down and explain to me what you're talking about." "You dialed the dead and I answered." "I dialed the number on this card," I replied and then pulled out the tarot card. "843-3323, the dead," She said. I pulled my cell phone. Sure enough the letters correspond with those numbers and the bones in my dream that said seek the dead.

"Well, Madam Discovery, maybe you can look into your crystal ball and tell me why my friend is dead and this card is the only evidence I have."

"Please, call me Miriam. Come sit at my table let me get to know you." I sat at the small round table across from Madame Discovery or Miriam as she asked to be called. "Now, tell Miriam all that troubles you." "I'll tell you what troubles me is dark forces have conjured up an evil spirit that has swooped down on my life like the wicked witch of the west. What troubles me are predators spreading fear and loathing throughout the streets of Jacksonville.

Slick and China Doll and so many beautiful lives have left this city at the hands of Villains like the Albino, the African and the Black Dread.

"What African is this you speak of; asked Miriam?" "A mother fucking death viper from the motherland that hurt my woman, struck a deadly blow to my best manz and even tried to kill me. He was last seen driving off in an old black hearse. My heart aches and my trigger finger itches for the opportunity to send him back to the hot dry dirt."

While rubbing her crystal ball, Miriam speaks, "You seek one who has made many suffer. He drives those who seek the dead. He possesses lethal venom."

"Tell me, Ms. Miriam. Where can I find him?" "Take A1A south to Saint Augustine," she said. "Thank you! Thank you, Ms. Miriam! What do I owe you?"

"It's been so long since I had a man in here, a strong viral man carrying such a big weapon." Ms. Miriam's eye's looked me up and down, but hers were not the only ones. A black cat was now staring at me from the floor next to her. A possum crawled up and sat on the back of her chair. Then on a wall shelf behind her appeared a raccoon. So, how about it? Break a sista off before you leave.

At this moment, I began to think of all the freaky shit I've done and how fucking this crazy Arab would be the icing on the cake. I can't help but wonder though if I pull out my dick, what will she do with it? Would she turn it into a squirrel or a catfish and feed it to that cat or that possum? "Another time, another place perhaps, Miriam, I've got a date with the devil. I can't be late."

"Sure, I understand, she said, it's just that my crystal ball tells me you would fuck me but you think I'm a crazy Arab." My mouth dropped open. I was so amazed at the accuracy of her glass ball. "Anyway, I'm a gypsy not an Arab. In case you haven't heard, gypsy gets what a gypsy wants."

Then from behind me out of the darkness that big Frankenstein jigga, Pastor Darryl appeared. He grabbed me from behind with his fish net sized hands and held me down in the chair with my arms pinned behind me. Ms. Miriam stood from her chair and like Houdini all her clothes fell to the floor. Revealing a slim hundred pound frame with water balloon shaped B-cup titties. Her body was all right but her face with its long nose and wart at the end was all wrong. She straddled herself over my chair then unzipped my pants. "So how about it cop, shoot me with your sex pistol", Ms Miriam said.

I wasn't aroused or amused by this spooky shit. My dick sprung up out of my pants anyway. I kept telling it to "stand down, stand down," but that bastard making mother fucker got a head of its own and doesn't listen to a word I say. She lines up the pussy and bungees herself down onto my dick. Ms. Miriam starts jumping up and down, pogo sticking my dick like it hand springs in it. I told him to stand down so he's getting just what he deserves but I got to get the fuck out of here. She's oohing, the cat and the raccoon are squealing and Pastor Darryl is singing, 'She's a gypsy woman.' It's time not just to pull out but to get out, like a one night stand you want to hit then split. I thrust up harder with my hips until I bounce her over the table. Pastor Daryl releases his grip and goes to her aid.

I zip up my pants and run for the car. I kicked up dust and dirt as I blasted from that black hole like the space shuttle. I jumped all three lanes of Beach Boulevard west bound. I hit the grassy median then snatched the steering wheel to the left. The Ferrari did a complete 360 degree turn. When the nose spun back east I floored it. Two streams of dirt and grass sprayed up behind me like water from my nitro powered black Jet Ski. I pushed myself snug into the driver's seat as I raced down the median at eighty miles per hour. I move over onto Beach Boulevard and could see the Atlantic Ocean from the top of the intercostals bridge. Just a mile from A1A it was clear I would go anywhere but back and nothing was going to keep me from getting him. If rain falls in buckets and fire scorches all the ground. If darkness and sorrow completely surround me, I'm still gonna be the son of a bitch that will go get the bad guy! The African could climb a mountain or jump a sea but from me he'll never be free.

I've got twenty five miles and about twenty minutes to St. Augustine. Although the only numbers that matter are the hours and days my enemy has to live. Instinct must tell him he's being tracked, that the predator has become the prey.

As I past the beautiful Oceanside scenery, I began to notice a fog cloud in my rearview mirror. Then I began to feel a slight dizziness. I shook my head from side to side to gain focus. As I shook my head, I caught a glimpse of a possum on the left side of the two lane highway. I don't know one possum from another but this looked like the possum from Ms. Miriam's. Another half mile then I saw a raccoon on the right side of the highway. I'm positive it's Ms. Miriam's raccoon. Aw man homey, my mind is playing tricks on me. I look in the rearview mirror and out of the fog appears Pastor Darryl and the two great Danes. He's waving me to come back.

Suddenly, I heard a loud screeching. I looked forward and saw the black cat in front of me but had no time to break before I hit it. I gathered my senses, pulled over then stopped. I got out of the car and walked back to the black cat. It was lying on its side in the middle of the road. Its head facing up with eyes and mouth open wide, full of terror, it decayed into a pile of maggots in just seconds, engulfed in the aroma of death. Ms. Miriam's voice rang out through the sky, "Come back! Come back!" My peace of mind was vexed; Ms. Miriam and her strange magic had a spell on me.

Last time I experienced anything like this I had smoked weed cured in acid and was running through Orange Park High school screaming and pulling out my hair. I ran to the car and from the glove compartment, I pulled my little green New Testament Bible and ran to the beach. I needed to talk to God. So, I wanted to see him face to face where the earth, ocean and sky meet.

At the tides edge about fifteen feet from a couple of sun tanning fishermen in beach chairs with coolers and salt water reels casting while they sip on Coronas. I open my little green Bible up to the Book of Psalms and read the twenty third psalm. I finished the chapter and closed with "God please be a hedge around me and protect me from all evil spirits, black cats, gypsies and their spells. Amen."

I put my little Bible in the left chest pocket of my black t-shirt then ran back to the car.

Good-bye, Ms. Miriam, hello St. Augustine. The sun is setting and the hunt for the African is on.

CHAPTER 22 – THE AFRICAN

LIKE A CRACK whoe tracking one last rock, I'm jones'n for the African and I don't think this can be settled until somebody gets smoked.

Saint Augustine, Florida, the nation's oldest city, at least that's what the sign says. Just then it starts to rain. I check to be sure my pistol is holstered tight, this may get grimy. Past the old jail and the Fountain of Youth, there's only one place I might find the type of person I'm looking for in this city, the Gully.

Saint Augustine's main trade center, the Gully consists of rows of eateries, candy shops, clothing and souvenir peddlers, hat shops and pottery barns. I parked the Ferrari in the nearest no parking spot I could find close to Saint George Street. I got out and headed up to the Gully. There was still a steady rain falling. I zipped my leather jacket all the way up trying to stay dry. Along the first block, I stopped in the Panama hat shop and bought one of those black fedora hats like the one Indiana Jones used to wear. I pulled it down on my head and continued along Saint George Street until I was drawn to a business advertising dream weavers. Seems like a good first stop to ask questions to me. I walk into the boutique of home made dream weavers, wind chimes, incense candles, and glass figurines.

"Hello," the petite fair skinned brunette in hippy clothes said.

"Hello, I love your shop. Lots of nice things and it smells good too."

"Thank you, she said, is there something special you're looking for?"

"Yes, there is. I'm trying to find someone in the area. He's an African, a real African with yellow eyes. Maybe you've seen him?" The little eclectic looking model said something that through me a loop. "Around here loose lips will get your dome split. If you understand what I'm saying?"

With water dripping from the lid of the fedora I replied, "Yes, I understand. All the bones buried round the Gully ain't old bones. The woman then raised her right arm and pointed towards the door. "Go and see the dead. There you'll find what you're seeking." "What do you mean," I said. "You must go and see the dead."

I walked out of the shop and continued along Saint George street past tourist and street vendors until I came upon a long bearded white guy with bushy red hair wearing a New York Yankee's Baseball jersey, white cotton boxer shorts, tan boat shoes and playing a saxophone. He was soaking wet, but playing that sax like he was on Bourbon Street at Mardi Gras. I stopped, then after several minutes; I eased up close between low notes then asked him where might I find the African? Without interrupting his tune, he pointed down to a large McDonald's cup on the ground next to him. I pulled a twenty, dropped it in the cup that contained coins and water. The sax man halted his playing then asked me, "Are you sure?" "Yes!" "Go down to the witch in the box. She'll show you the Mumbler. He'll lead you to the African." There was something convincing about what he said even though it sounded like a bunch of bullshit. I dropped another twenty in the cup then started off. In the rain, I walked to the third building. I came upon an open corridor with a sign overhead that read fortune row. I stepped in and walked down the corridor of coin operated amusement venders. Penny press machines that make charms, handshake machines that tell your personality, palm reading machines that tell if you'll be rich and famous.

Then there she was in a glass casing on top a wooden box. The witch was an old white woman with long stringy grey hair, missing teeth and a long crooked nose, a dollar for my fortune, huh? What the hell, I slid the bill into the receptor and pressed my birth sign. The case lit up and the witch's hands move over a stack of tarot cards. A small piece of paper slid from an opening in the box. "You'll find your future behind you," the paper read. The witch's hands stopped moving then the lights in the box went dark. "What the hell?" I was about to walk away when a reflection in the glass caught my eye. Across the corridor, behind me was a statue of full medieval armor with shield and sword. It stood in front of a medieval weapons and armor souvenir shop. Eighteenth and nineteenth century gangster shit. As I started to move past it, the statue of armor spoke, "Did you say something?" I asked the statue. The statue replied in a muffled, mangled monolog.

The Mumbler! It had to be, I couldn't understand shit he was saying. The future was behind me, but how could I know what it was.

I reached up and lifted the iron helmet from his head. "Thanks, man!" the sweaty, flush faced white kid said. "I'm looking for someone."

"Who," the kid asked.

"An African, a real African" I answered.

"What's it worth," he replied. I pulled a couple of twenties. "Go out the back, then to your left. Follow the street to the cemetery. Across the street you will find him. He labors for the dead." I put the twenties between his teeth and place the iron helmet back on his head then walked out. I walked a quarter mile along the back street to an old historic cemetery with graves hundreds of years old, across the street from the cemetery, a sign, Welcome to The Dead Inn.

At the end of a short driveway was an old three story hotel. In front of the hotel sat an old black hearse. Standing there between the two rear doors was the African! Even through the rain, I could see his yellow eyes. A sign near the hearse reads, 'Dead Tours, visit ghost and graves.' He was about 5'11" tall wearing baggy black jeans and t-shirt. There was a skull and cross bone design on the t-shirt. He's got several silver chains with crosses hanging from his neck. He's loaded his passengers and run around to the driver's side while I splashed my way through water puddles to reach the rear door before he could pull off. I sat on the third row of the hearse. Seeing him alive brings back all the emotion of Slick's death. My eyes tear up and I can barely contain myself. It takes every bit of restraint I have not to lunge at him. Don't rush this C.J., don't rush this, I keep telling myself. He turns in his seat and asks everyone to pass forward their $30 fee for the tour, the four other passengers and myself (one in the front and three on the second row). My hat is pulled down barely revealing my eyes and the water dripping from the brim, but the African still pauses to stare at me on the third row. He must have recognized me. Don't rush, C.J., don't rush. "I am called Mamba!" The African says. "Hello, Mamba!" The other riders respond. I could call Detectives Biscuit and Jelly. They'll come with a swat team and throw a net over this spear chunker, but I'm not. I swear to God and Slick, he's going down. I'm going to take him.

Our thirty minute tour is now over. The last tourist has left the hearse. With his yellow eyes looking at me in the rear view mirror he says, "You look like the bad guy in all that black." "I can be, if it's called for," I respond.

"I like this lil' job, riding people around showing them graves and ghosts. It helps me take care of my woman and little boy who came to this country with me."

"I've even started going to church, believe it or not I sit on the front row. I've changed; although there's something's I did I can't take back." "Yeah, I said; we all change and move from place to place. We can get away from homes, neighborhoods, relatives. We just can't get away from the consequences. You sit on the front row, but you belong on death row," I told the African. "The consequences of our actions always catch up with us. One day, we're driving along through life without a care in the world, and then next thing you know in the rearview mirror you see your consequences sitting in the back seat".

"America has given me a good life."

"Well, she wants it back and I'm here to take it."

"I came to this country an heir to the throne of Mozambigue, an African prince, a descendant of great and good people."

"Well sometimes the streets make good people go bad. Sometimes hard times make good people go bad. Sometimes people are just bad, and then a person like me has to come get them," I told the African. "It's reaping time. My Friend Slick was full of large caliber bullet holes. What you know about that?" I ask. "I've laid a few cats down. I'm nice with the long barrel. So, maybe you give me a chance to have a little prayer before this all goes down," he asks. "Take your time I told him, I'll give a man that."

The African then bowed his head then began to whisper what sounded like a prayer. "Amen," I heard as his head raised and those yellow eyes looked at me in the rearview mirror. This time he spoke in a harder voice, "I ain't had nothing against your boy. We were bitches for another motherfucker. Some cash, some coke, some Viagra and we was showed the location on map quest then told to take care of the jigga's that showed up. You were late. You were the main mark."

"Why me god dammit," I screamed from the back row.

"You have vexed the beast and stolen the crown jewel from the temple. He has called for your flesh on the Alter."

"What does that mean? Who sent you?" I yelled at the African.

"I'm an African prince, down with the voodoo gang. I ain't no rat or snitch! So, let me re-introduce myself. I'm Mamba, Black Mamba, the Mozambique mobster, welcome to Killville."

His words rang out in slow motion compared to the speed he used to reach into his clothing and pull his weapon. Even before he turned, I could see his right arm extending holding the long barrel pistol with the red beam scope in his hand. All that talk of church and changing his life, if he had joined the church he was back sliding fast and I needed to do something quick or I would be the topic of his next confession. As his arm swung around the red beam of light moved along the inside of the vehicle towards me.

The 357 magnum he held started to spark fire and spit shells. I pulled my blue steel ooee and fell over in the seat. He kept blasting. I reached up over the second row seat then bust back with duce fours. The Afro verses the American. The 357 verses the 44 magnum. The Anti-Christ verses the Christ. The smoke, the noise, glass fragments and the ricocheting bullets, we both got down on the floor of the vehicle with arms up firing off shots that we hoped will hit. Our weapons emptied almost the same time. We kept pulling the trigger just in case.

We both sprung up and threw our weapons at each other. His gun grazed my head and knocked off my new fedora. My 44 hit the rearview mirror and broke it from the windshield. He lunged out the passenger door. I was right behind him. The African was running, cutting corners and ripping through yards like a baby antelope and I was on his ass like a cheetah.

Back alleys, narrow side roads, then into the old cemetery, we were running through the grave yard in the pitch dark. That African was hurdling tombstones like Hamon Moses and I was dipping, leaning, gripping and kicking up dirt right behind him. Hard grunts with wet clothes flapping in the wind, I never saw the small statue of the Spanish conquistador before I ran head on into it. I fell but was up quickly.

The African had gained distance but his silhouette was in sight. He ran to a small building at the rear of the cemetery. I could see it was some sort of Mortuary building. I charge through the door and ran chest first into the large metal tomb in the middle of the small room. Behind me as I turned around is the African. He pulled two folding straight razors, and then began swinging them at me in cris-crossing movements. I moved back as he slashed and cut my leather jacket as if his hands were eagle talons. Atop the metal tomb was a two foot high bronze cross which I grabbed and swung at the African. He surprised me with a side kick that knocked me to the floor. "Death to you by Black Mamba," he said. Then turned and ran out the building.

Outside, I didn't see him but I followed the sound I heard coming from the rear of the building. There was the African climbing over a six foot metal fence. The fence separated the back of the cemetery from swampy woodlands and was marked with signs that said danger keep out. He disappeared into the thick trees and plants. I ran to the fence, pulled myself up and leaped over. I hit the ground and sank into about six inches of mud. Maybe this was more to the African's liking but no matter the battlefield, I can't let him get away. I plunged one foot after the other through the thick mud while weaving my way through ferns, banana plants and black water.

The water gets deeper as I follow the Africans path into the swamp. The deeper water is an obstacle course of tree stumps, hanging limbs and swamp frogs. Even with my ears still ringing from the gunfire I can hear the African ahead although my eyes focused on the blinking eyes dotting the surface of the water. Dozens of pairs, every eye on me while the splashing of the African was being drowned out by the splashes all around me. I'm now treading through about three feet of water. The eyes seem to be grouping together and moving along at the same pace I was. A fear came over me at that moment. With all the strength I could gather, I was taking long high strides jumping up and through the water. The faster I went the faster the eyes pursued. 'This can't be! How could it?' I strode higher and faster and began to say what any jigga in this situation would say, "Jesus! Lord, have mercy, Jesus! Jesus! Help me, Jesus!"

Then ahead, I could see a light about fifteen yards. Could it be Jesus? He had come to my rescue. Jesus! I yelled louder, Jesus, Help me, Jesus! As I leaped from the water with every stride the eyes would converge on my last. I was nearing the light and the water's getting shallower, seven yards away. It was a light bulb over a small black and white sign. The sign read, 'Alligators, Don't feed.' Son of a bitch! Not only did the African bring me through the back of the Alligator Farm, but the Alligators have not been fed.

Jesus! Help me, Jesus! I was nearing the edge of the large swamp pond with gators snapping at my ass like I was Bobby Bowden. Just a few strides off shore, I decide the time was right to long jump. With one massive leap I exit the water. Both arms and legs extended in front of me. It was an incredible leap. The gators and the frogs watched in amazement as I glided through the air as if Jesus had really come and given me wings. I would not feed the gators today! Then I hit the embankment and was quick sanded in three feet of mud. Fuck! Help me, Jesus! Help me!

Help me Jesus, look past my faults and see my needs. If I wasn't standing in this mud I'd be on my knees begging you please. I shouted as the alligators reach the water's edge lining up with jaws snapping and making hissing sounds as they started to march from the water. The gators marched forward while I struggle to free my legs from the mud then looked wide right and there was the African five yards away in the same predicament. Thigh deep in mud trying not to become a two piece dinner with a side order of mud pie, I remember my 22 caliber short holstered in my groin. I quickly zipped down my pants, reaching to pull the silver lining from the clouds and took aim. I started firing, hitting gators between the eyes turning savage reptiles into roles of shoe and belt fabric. Gators fell back to the tide. I fired the gun 'til it was empty then threw the gun down the throat of one of the hungry reptiles.

The African was now free. "I guess I owe you for holding off the gators?" he said. "Damn right you owe!" "Black Mamba lets no debt go unpaid." He then reached into his front pocket and pulled a ten inch switch blade. He threw it striking me in the chest, a bull's eye to the heart. Time stopped as I reached up with both hands grabbing the handle of the switch blade. I tugged at the blade which had only lodged itself deep into the little green Bible I had placed in my shirt pocket at the ocean side. I pulled the blade from the Bible. "Thank you, Jesus! Thank you for helping me!" The African lunged for the top of the embankment, but in the thick chocolate milkshake mud he began to slide down towards the water. The Alligators had regrouped for another charge. I was able to slide my feet out of my shoes then use the flat side of the blade to pull myself up out of my pants to firmer ground. Mean while, the African slowly slid down the muddy bank to the waters edge. As his frantic grasps kept coming up with slippery slush he called out, "Jesus! Help me too, Jesus!" I looked back at his decent into the waiting mob of gators.

"Unless you're Tebow you better call on somebody you know," I yelled to him. He continued to scream as the gators began to devour him up, forearm, a foot, a thigh, an arm, screaming 'til his last breath. I pulled myself up over the bank. Looking down into the pond as the smaller gators finished up the scraps.

"You may have been a warrior, a prince or future king back in your country, But around these parts of Northeast Florida, You're either Gator or you're Gator bate, Justice for Slick; Justice for China Doll and Justice for Rosa. Yes Black Mamba, Justice done come." It stopped raining.

CHAPTER 23 – GOOD PUSSY

I FOUND A TREE stump outside the fence that surrounds the gator pond. I sat there looking at the few shredded strips of clothing left by the alligators at the waters edge. I want to feel something for the African. What I feel inside is the feeling I get when I have something to do with anyone dieing. There's a moment when the world seems a little bit lonelier. It passes then I'm glad it was that jigga and not me.

The Albino and the African were mere branches on the tree. I've got to get to the root, and see how deep he's planted in this contaminated ground. I got to find the Black Dread. First though, I must get my pants out of this mud. My cell phone and car keys are in the pockets. But after watching those gators snack on the African, I'm definitely not going inside that fence. I sat on the stump in my underwear, t-shirt and ripped up leather jacket covered in mud.

As I sat devising a plan to get my pants, the gators lined up at water's edge. "Sir?" an humble voice spoke from behind. I looked to see an even humbler looking middle aged man about six feet, four inches tall and rail thin. He's got a small oval head with a long nose. He's wearing khaki green short pants, short sleeved shirt with ankle high canvas boots. The shirt has the words Alligator Farm written on the left front pocket. "Sir," he says looking puzzled at my circumstance, "Gator Park is closed." "I'm trying to leave, I told him, but my pants are in that mud."

He moved up to the four foot fence looking at my pants, the platoon of alligators and me in my boxers covered in mud. "Sir, he says again, you shouldn't mess with them gators." "Believe me I know, but how are we going to get my pants? I'm sorry. I didn't introduce myself. I'm C.J." "Hey, Mr. C.J., I go by the name Lambcharles." "Well, pleased to meet you, Mr. Lambcharles." Lambcharles walked to a large aluminum storage building then came back with a long adjustable tree limb cutter. He reached over the fence and pulled the pants from the mud. "Thank you, Mr. Lambcharles." "Sir, them gators mean. You should go out the front." "I sure will." I took my pants from the end of the pole, thanked him again and followed the exit signs.

Back at the Ferrari, I removed the illegal parking tickets and decided I would spend the night in Saint Augustine. Then I would visit my kids and ex-wife in Palencia the next day. I pulled into a bed and breakfast off US1. A little place named Debbie and Al's B&B. I paid for a night plus extra soap, shampoo and towels. I called to check on Rosa and let her know I was spending the night. Then I called Detective Biscuit to tell him I caught up with the African but got only bits and pieces and last I saw him he was feeding the alligators. After a nice long cleansing shower, I sat on the side of the bed thinking over my next move.

With my next thought, I woke the following morning face down in the nude with my head between two pillows. All my muscles ached as I turned and stepped on the floor. The operators of the B&B served up a fabulous homemade breakfast while my clothes washed in their laundry room. I tipped my host and left with no more answers than I came with. However, I was leaving it a safer place than when I came.

I pulled onto US1 starting my twenty minute drive west to Palencia. My alimony and child support payments allow my ex-wife and kids to live in this upscale township. Even though Jackie and I are divorced, we still want the best for each other and the children.

She was my college sweetheart, a beautiful dark brown tribute to the perfect female form. We lived life as if we were just vacationing on earth for the weekend. After college we married. Even with two kids, our flame still burned hot. I'd patrol the night for the force then she and I would roam the night with a force. It was all under control 'til the smoke got in her nose. Addicts will tell you, whether passing or on purpose, that first hit and you're hooked. Crack pipes hidden in make-up cases, sofa cushions and car seats. Street corner connects for nickel and dime pieces. All that powder needed was the hot flame from our passion to ignite a bomb under our relationship. Besides, I had my own jones going on, side sex. Roaming for bootie like a serial killer looking for someone's throat to cut, prowling the concrete jungle mauling whoes like a Jacksonville Jaguar. The fireworks from both our cannons left the relationship mortally wounded. But like a strong black sister, she kicked it and pulled her life together. My wisdom had not grown to the level of my lust. In my search for good pussy, I lost my marriage; two years, two kids and too many transgressions.

I made my turn off US 1 onto the main road into downtown Palencia. It's time for soccer practice, so I'll go directly to the ball park. I quickly reached the acres of miniature soccer fields and there they are. Pure joy smothered me seeing them test their running and kicking skills in their bright blue and yellow uniforms. The coach, a black guy, was about my age. He manages the team well. I looked across the field. Jackie and I are eye to eye. She's the best looking woman here, bra top, blue jeans with platform sandals. She was a Victoria secret model with a high top bootie. Her best friend Sandy was with her. Sandy was the complete opposite, about 5 feet 5 inches, 180 pounds and she wore her hair in a short neat afro. They play tennis, golf and bowl together. Sandy rides a motorcycle and smokes little cigars. I don't understand them being close but women need friends. Had I not been looking at that spot across the field, I might not have noticed the small black helicopter hovering in the distance. Is someone watching or is it just the cop in me. I looked down to see both kids racing towards me, "daddy daddy" yelled Tamira; my four year old and little CJ, my six years old. I knelt down catching one in each arm. I hit the kid kissing lottery. "Daddy can we have pizza now?" "You're not done with the game." "We want pizza!" "Well, let's walk over and talk to your mother." The coach had already sent replacement players onto the field. I could hardly take my eyes off Jackie as we walked around the field, except for glancing up at the damn helicopter. "Hello, Jackie!" my mouth spoke but my heart said 'I'm sorry.' I'm sorry we didn't make it for better and for worse. I'm sorry for not being there for knee scrapes, tummy aches and ice cream and cake. I'm sorry you're another strong black women left alone. I wanted to say all that but what came out was, "How about pizza?" Jackie and Sandy laughed and the kids yelled, "Yes, we're going for pizza!" I followed them to the local pizza parlor. During college, it was Jackie's and I Friday night ritual: pizza, a movie, then sex.

The five of us laughed and enjoyed our pizza and soda. Sandy fit right in. I don't know her very well. I knew she was a massage therapist who moved to the area three years ago from Knoxville, Tennessee. The kids played with their complementary games. Jackie filled me in on as much of their daily activity as we could get in. Soon the pizza was done and we were all back at Jackie's watching kid's cartoons till bed time. I tucked the kids in with a prayer and a kiss.

Coming down the hallway from the kids' room, I pass Jackie's room. Through the opened door, I see her lying in the middle of the bed with her head resting on several pillows. Her hair is rapped in a red, black and green African print scarf. She's wearing a thigh length emerald green satin pencil strap nightie. Jackie's body screamed sex no matter the position. She was the visual cure for erectile dysfunction. I stopped. Our eyes connected. I walked into the room to a small woven basket filled with skin creams and body lotions. I took out a purple tube, popped the top and squirted a hand full then sat on the side of the bed and began to lotion and rub her feet. "Jackie, its days like this that make me want to turn all my wrongs into rights," I said. "But you could never put us first before. Why should I believe anything's changed? There's always going to be criminals and you're always going to want to catch them," Jackie said in a low tone. "It's in my blood, Jackie! I'm the antidote to these jiggaz venom." "But there's an entire police force, CJ. It is not just you!" "The kids miss me terribly and to be honest I believe that's why you haven't gotten another man. Take tonight for example." "What do you mean?" "You know what I mean. You all up in here with this little bit of fabric on and I don't believe you're wearing panties either." "What are you trying to say?" "I know the look of love when I see it and there ain't but one man in here." "CJ, there's something I need to tell you." "Jackie, I don't need details. We both grown and we've been apart for so long. You need a man who can do the job. Let me get an interview."

That's when Sandy opened the bathroom door. Standing there in the same emerald green nightie Jackie was wearing except six sizes larger. I looked at Sandy, Sandy looked at Jackie, and Jackie looked at me. Sandy looked at me and said, "Dog, you got to find your own bitch." I looked at

Jackie, Jackie looked at Sandy, and Sandy looked at Jackie. Jackie turned to me and said, "But I tried to tell you." Sandy cut off the bathroom light then went to the dresser at the left side of the room. She lit a candle then another on the night stand next to the bed. As she moved around the room I could see her big girl stomach pouch hanging down. Sandy cut off the bedroom light then grabbed her hanging stomach pooch and shook it at me. "What you looking like that for, she said, it's some good pussy under here. Now get out of here and don't dilly dally! Next time, play your cards right pimp and you won't find yourself in this situation." I looked at Sandy, Sandy looked at me, I looked at Jackie, and Jackie just shrugged her shoulders.

I stood up not sure what to do or say next then walked out of the bedroom and pulled the door, but not all the way. I walked a couple of steps then moon walked backwards to the crack in the door. With their bodies barely visible in the candle light, I could see Sandy pull her emerald green nightie over her head and drop it to the floor. Then Jackie pulled hers off. Sandy was thick with big titties, a fat ass and that stomach pooch. Sandy got into bed and the two lay facing each other. Rubbing nipples and twirling their tongues together like two snakes dancing. Then kissing one another's nipples and twisting their legs together like a couple of professional wrestlers. Jackie lay on her back and Sandy crawled on top. Then something happen that's rarely seen by the heterosexual male. It was the sacred lesbian ritual of bumping pussy. I pressed my eye harder into the little opening. If someone closed the door, I'd walk around the rest of my life with an eye patch. For a good six minutes that big dyke pounded Jackie's pussy. I start to get an erection, here kitty kitty. Looks like they got a nice little quinella working, but my dick wants to play a trifecta. I think it's too late to get my horse in the race, sandy's already won by a nose. What happened next was as gripping as watching a priest masturbate. Sandy paused from her pussy pounding to reach over and open the top drawer of the nightstand on the right side of the bed. Without looking she seemed to know just what she was seeking. She pulled an object from the drawer and held it in the palm of her hand as she slid down Jackie's body and between her legs. She rubbed her tongue across Jackie's body all the way down.

Like spreading icing on a hot cinnamon bun. She licked her from her nappy 'fro to her camel toe. Jackie spread her legs and bent her knees. I could see Sandy's left arm go under Jackie's right thigh then reach up and hold her right breast. Her right hand revealed a small black five inch vibrator about as round as my thumb. With one hand she cut it on then slowly slid it in Jackie's pussy. I could hear the low hum under Jackie's moaning. Like a real veteran, Sandy began a slow gentle probing. What she did next separates men from the boys or the girls from the boys or the lesbians from the boys or whatever. While continuing her slow in and out penetration with the vibrator she began to apply a little flick action to the clit with her tongue. Jackie's right hand reached up and gripped the bed post. Her left hand palmed the back of Sandy's head. After a few minutes her entire body tensed up and began to shake like a death row inmate being electrocuted. Pussy foaming up like a root beer float, then with one big exhale she gave up the ghost and went limp.

Damn! I wanted to get mad or jealous or something but that was a masterful piece of work. Damn! She must have gone to school to learn that. It all ended with them wrapping their bodies into one ball of warm, moist flesh. I don't understand it all, but they seem happy with each other. Having somebody who'll stay when the easy loving is over and the hard living begins.

I pause to think whom better than a woman to teach a man what good pussy is really all about. That pussy you're getting the day you decide to stop looking, to stop chasing, to stop hound-dogging. When you decide to hold it till you become one ball of flesh. Wow! That's good pussy!

CHAPTER 24 – CENTURION JUSTICE

KISS MY STILL sleeping kids on their cheeks at 6:00am and left a note and three grand for Jackie. I purposely got out before her and Sandy woke up. Not because everybody got some pussy but me, I just wasn't sure what I'd say to them. I said in my note that I loved her and the kids and I would be back soon to spend time with the four of them.

With little traffic I had time to reflect, you don't have to chase pussy and be married. Pussy is just one treat. Marriage is a gift basket with candy, fruit, flowers and the treat. It's always got something good to eat. Next time I commit, I'll truly commit.

I'm back in Jacksonville with time to catch Bootleg Keith and pick up some tunes. I turn onto Hendricks Avenue then pull up to the little breakfast spot for the dread heads called the Lollipop.

Right out in front in his usual spot is Bootleg Keith. At a small round table holding court over the bootleg movies and CD's he sells. If the brothers got news he'll sell that too. You have to be careful though. Everything he sells is a little scratchy, especially his news. "What's up, Keith?" Bootleg Keith in his powder blue sweat suit with sky blue bandana around his head halla's back. What up cool breeze?" Bootleg Keith calls everybody cool breeze. "I'm on my grind, Keith. But you know every super hero needs his own theme music. So, what you got?" "I got some old school R&B, rap, some jazz." "I want four R&B, four rap and two jazz. Whoever is hot." "No worries, Cool Breeze. I got what you need." "I need something else."

"What is it?"

"I need to know where I can find a bad ass dread jigga with a gold grill that's into voodoo."

Keith's fear factor awoke, "You said you where looking for music, but you looking to get a jigga killed." "So, what can you tell me?"

"I can tell you, that's an unspeakable evil and the CD's will be fifty bucks."

"I want that turd, I don't care how hard you got to strain to give him up. Here's two hundred and fifty bucks. Now sing me a song with that."

Keith took the two fifty from my hand then quickly looked around making sure he wasn't heard. He leaned in closer and in a low voice said, "Hog Farm."

"What?" I replied.

"Hog Farm, find it, you find the dread."

"Are you kidding me, a Hog Farm?

"That's right, I know for a fact that he's got a deal with the devil. Now unless you want to buy some movies, I suggest you move on." "Sure thing, Keith, but if any of what I've paid for ain't quality, I'll be back for a refund." "If it gets out I spoke about him I'll end up slop for them hogs.

I pulled off and in minutes I'm parking on river road in front of the apartment. Inside I opened up China Doll's file; the only female victim of this rampage. What's up with that? She's got a story and I need to hear it! I called the medical assistant staffing company she worked for and spoke with Ms. Abi Pamolis the manager. She said I could come by and talk about China Doll or as they know her Natalie Parks. I ate breakfast with Rosa while studying over the pictures I had of Natalie with her mother and brother.

After breakfast Rosa left for the Spa and I go to the bedroom and kneel down at the bed. I should have prayed but instead I pull from underneath the bed the only thing I left the force with, a shoe box containing a badge, a hand full of letters of commendation and my formal dismissal for actions unbecoming of an officer of law enforcement.

That's what I walked out of the building with, a shoebox, Me, the big bust brother who couldn't be bought, Me, the lunch with the mayor and golf with the city council president, Me, black tie formal and closed door official. I was 'the shit' and they asked me to leave with just 'the shit' in this box.

I held onto these things like a divorced man not willing to give up his wedding band. I was unfaithful to Jacksonville and she put me out. But she's still the heart inside my chest. She did what she had to do. She will always be my city, my hustle, my flow. I'll get her back. After a quick shower and shave, I wrapped myself in a black one button Versace suit with a long sleeve black silk shirt, a pair of black J.M. Weston wingtips and slid the files into my black Johnston Murphy briefcase and peeled out in the black Ferrari.

Over the Mathews Bridge, I exited Park Street to the Five Points area, down St. Johns Ave across from St. George's Hospital. I entered the door of suite 103, Medical Assistant Staffing Company. I was greeted by a cute young Brunette named Jennifer. I showed her my badge and told her I was here to see Ms. Pamolis. She phoned to notify her then offered me coffee or water. I waited just a couple of minutes when a middle aged blonde wearing a navy blue pants suit entered the waiting area. She quickly approached me with her hand extended. "Detective Justice?" She asked. "Hello," I said, while shaking her hand and flashing my old detective badge, "Yes Justice, Centurion Justice."

"Pleased to meet you Mr. Justice, so the police department is continuing the pursuit of Natalie's killer?" "I've sounded for the trumpet that will never sound retreat. The killer will be found and justice will prevail, I promise." "Well, thank you Mr. Justice. How can I help you?" "I'm hoping to learn more about Natalie and what brought her to that last day." "Follow me", Ms. Pamolis said as she turned. I followed her through a door then down a hallway past cubicles occupied by mostly young women working at computers. I followed here to a small office. She sat behind the desk and I in front.

She spoke of Natalie as sincerely as a mother speaking of her child. "She was a precious gift to the world," She said. "It was truly a savage and barbaric act, I told her, but is there anything to suggest Natalie was targeted and not a victim of random violence." "No, Natalie was the type of woman men would do wrong for, not wrong to." Ms. Pamolis then pulled from her purse a picture of Natalie with a ring on a silver chain around her neck. "She wore a promise ring her father gave her around her neck. Natalie had a heart full of grace and truly loved helping others." "She was a child of

God, someone is going to pay in this life or the next if they don't repent." "Repent my ass, I responded; whoever did this will pay in this life and the next!" "But Mr. Justice, Jesus saves." "Yes he does, but he can save it for later cause this person's ass is mine."

Just then Ms. Pamolis pulled from her desk drawer a Chinese American newspaper article. The article was about the exceptional efforts of a young detective to take down gangs in his Chinese city. The chiseled features, the close cut hair. All the pictures I had seen of Natalie's family were of a younger man with longer hair. There it is! The past has brought me clarity in the present. He was the lean muscular silhouette from Rosa's bedroom window, the chiseled muscular brother crossing the street at the strip club killings, the dude on the bus after I took down the Albino. I barely noticed him. "That's Natalie's brother, Ms. Pamolis confirmed, I'm surprised you haven't met him. He said he would be working Natalie's case as a joint effort between the two law enforcement agencies." "When did you talk to him?" I asked her. "When he picked up copies of Natalie's files and e-mails?"

"He was here?"

"Yes, shortly after Natalie's death."

"Ms. Pamolis, I need copies of the files and e-mails you gave him." "Certainly, but is there something wrong, Mr. Justice?" "Yes, I've got to tighten up my game."

I stood and thanked her then ran to my car. What's my hurry? Where am I going? Who am I chasing? A guy working a case with false authorization; Hell! so am I. If China Doll's brother killed these guys out of revenge for the death of his loved one, what am I going to do about it? Hell! So am I. Should I find him and give him more bullets, a sharper knife? I pulled out of the parking lot racing downtown to the police headquarters to search the Interpol world police intelligence listings. I need background on China Doll's brother. How long has he been on the prowl in my city? How long has the tiger been chasing the same prey as the lion?

The stop light caught me at the five points shopping strip. I could see the Ferrari's reflection in the big glass window of the little jewelry store. At that moment the sun's rays shifted, striking the big brilliant cut crystal on display in the show case. I pulled to the curve and ran inside the shop. No second thought necessary, I love what I see in Rosa. She's an insatiable dish, I can never get a huge without wanting a kiss. It's time to put a ring on it. I gave the clerk the black card and she gave me the black box.

At the police headquarters, Detective Jelly met me as I exited the second floor elevator. "Justice!" in a stern voice he said, "I received a call from the St. Augustine police department! What do you know about a shootout and a chase involving two black males about your size and shreds of clothing found in a pond at the St. Augustine Alligator Farm?" "Well, I'm now a Florida State Seminole Fan and I won't be going swimming for a while." "You don't kill anybody else around here without a note from me! You got that?" "I don't suppose you could write me out one now. When the situation arises time is of the essence." "Don't be a smartass, Justice!" The detective held up a picture and tells me it's the sketch their artist made from the bus driver's description of the man sitting across from Big Balls Barber Shop. I held up the article with China Doll's brother picture. "It's a pretty good resemblance wouldn't you say." "Who is he?" asked Detective Jelly. "Let's get to a computer and find out."

Using Detective Biscuit's security clearance, I logged on to the world law enforcement cite of Interpol. I put in his name and it immediately gave me the anti-crime division for Shanghai, China. There elite crime fighters are listed as agent zeros. I pulled up his profile. Michael Parks, age 27. He's busted everything from prostitution rings to drug smugglers. His nickname is 'Boy Sheriff of Shanghai.' He specializes in martial arts, but is an expert marksman.

In J's-Ville, the boy sheriff must answer to the man, Centurion Justice. The boys good though. What's next? Who's next? If Bootleg Keith's information was correct. All roads led to the Hog Farm. All roads led to the Black Dread!

CHAPTER 25 – VOODOO NEGRO ZOMBIE

THE ACTIVITY IN the police headquarters began to stir up like an espresso machine. Officers scurrying around the room for their bullet proof vests and extra weapons. Word of trouble snaked through the room till it reached Detectives Biscuit and Jelly. "What's going on?" I asked Biscuit as he prepared to roll out. Popcorn dead!

"They just found Popcorn dead!"

"Who's Popcorn?"

"One of our best; a real up and comer not long out the academy but already making his mark. He reminds a lot of people around here of you when you came on board," Jelly replied. "Oh, and one more thing, Jelly said, he's the cop we had posted in front of Rosa's place."

I don't remember getting from my chair to the sidewalk in front of the police memorial building, just me sliding across the hood of the Ferrari then firing it up and blasting off down Bay Street. I press down on the gas peddle 'til the speedometer reads fuck the limit then fishtailed all over the Main Street Bridge. If this car could fly I still couldn't get there fast enough. "Jesus! Jesus! Be there 'til I get there." I pulled my cell phone then dialed Rosa's number as I formula one'd along the short side streets. No answer! I turned onto River Road. It's lined with Jacksonville Sheriff's office police cars. I stopped my car in front of the apartment and blocked the street.

All eyes on me, good cop, bad cop, they're all here. Once you take out one of theirs, then they're coming to kill you. I leap from the car just in front of the dead cop's car. Looking through the windshield, I could see the young man's head turned toward his right shoulder with a stream of blood from his left temple. Coroners and evidence technicians standing around the driver's door, I reached the apartment door never feeling more violated. "Please, Jesus," I quietly said to myself as I closed my eyes and opened the door.

My eyes opened to a room full of police officers. "Fuck!" I glanced around and Rosa is nowhere in sight. "Where is she?"

"The surveillance target is not here," responded one of the officers.

"She's not a target! I said, she's Rosa, she's my woman and I should have been here. I don't mean to lash out at you. You just don't know her. You don't know her walk, her voice, her scent, her passion or the love she has for me. You don't know her style or the way she makes me smile. How her love blossomed for me even when I didn't water it. She's got the key to my heart and ain't no spare. Where is she?"

"She wasn't here when we arrived," said the muscular officer wearing S.W.A.T. team gear. "We did find a broken chain lock, some signs of a struggle, that picture on the living room floor and a blue contact lens." It was a six inch by nine inch picture of Rosa taken from the living room table. A closer look reveals a large caliber bullet positioned on top of Rosa's face. "That's the way we found it. The evidence technician has to collect these items for DNA testing. One more thing, he said, follow me." I followed him through the apartment to the bathroom. There in big red lipstick on the bathroom mirror, 'Eye for Eye, Queen for Queen' with the word CHAOS as a signature underneath. "We're not sure what it means, do you?" "It's fuck'n on! That's what it means!"

"Mr. Justice, we're going to dig like gopher turtles and track like blood hounds until we find who did this." "You go ahead and do what you got to do with your turtles and hounds. I'm going to open up skulls until I find Rosa and the answer to all this killing. Who is this CHAOS?" I asked the officer. "He's a dark black Jamaican with a heart to match. He wears long dreads, a gold mouth grill and he's into Voodoo shit." "Why hasn't he gone down?" "He's a ghost, said the officer. He's been impossible to catch and people on the street are afraid to speak his name not to mention testify against him. He was known to hang with an Albino and an African." "Is there anything else?" I asked the officer. "A neighbor reported seeing a big black Mercedes with black window tint leaving the scene." I left the bathroom and went to the closet then pulled the tool box. I walked out of the apartment down the sidewalk to my car.

Every officer paused to watch me walk by. This was one case I wouldn't need a note to kill somebody. The looks on their faces told me I had the green light. I put the tool box on the passenger seat then pulled off as if I knew just where to find Rosa. I do know my next stop is Nubbie's, the street information terminal. Driving moncrief road to downtown, traveling through the bombed out, shot up parts of Soulville. All the while passing cop cars that are pulling over every vehicle with big rims and tinted windows. Two words will get every Brother in this town strip searched; Cop Killer. When a cop gets killed you shake up the streets 'til the gang banging thugs give up the jigga you need.

At Richardson Road, I past the iron gates of DC Heights Apartment that are being patrolled by young drug sentinels. Jiggaz so young they barely got pubic hair but already shaving, shaving cocaine. These sprite and baking soda cooking slayers are known as the cake boys. Just across the street is a vacant lot where an old fashioned tent revival is being held. How ironic, the kids are selling rock and the parents are calling on the rock. The only thing that separates heaven or hell is the turn lane. How many generations of young blacks are we going to lose to neglect? Black community leaders ask who's going to feed them, clothe them, house them, educate and nurture them. What the fuck you mean who! That same jigga who's dick dug them up out that whoe's ass, that's who. Throw a plow around his neck and get to get'n.

I reach Nubbie's, walk in and the joint is jumping with all the regulars, Earl, Atlanta, Cant-chance-it and maybe ten others trying to talk over the jukebox and grease frying in the kitchen. I squeeze up to the counter and see Nubbie sitting in his chrome wheelchair reading the sports page.

The stool next to me empties and quickly a thick leg, fat ass cutie sat down. She told me her name was Flossy and she knew my reputation. "How about us going around to the bar and you buy me a drink?" "Flossy, you're fishing without a pole right now! I got business to take care of." Nubbie heard me shoot her down, knowing me that got his attention. He looked up from his paper then said, "If you're not a lover then you're a fighter, who you looking to fight Centurion?" "Chaos," I answered. What happened next is hard to believe. The entire restaurant went silent. Everyone stopped talking and I swear the jukebox stopped playing. Nubbie gestured for me to come down to the end of the counter. I leaned over to hear him clearly. Before he spoke he gave a stern hard look around the restaurant. All the patrons began to mingle again, hell, even the music started to play again.

"Justice, he said, the Dread is the kind of guy you fuck with and you wish all you had was Aids." A voice behind me says, "He's a cold hearted snake." I turn and it's Cant-chance-it talking over my shoulder. "What do you know about him?" I ask. "I know he's an evil truth, locked in mystery, rapped in a puzzle, and hidden in a maze."

"Tell me, Cant-chance-it, where can I find him?" "You can find him in legend. A boy born to a Jamaican hooker, still turning tricks the night she gave birth to him on a bus stop bench. With the placenta still hanging, she took thirty dollars from a John for anal sex then road off leaving him on the bus stop bench. He was taken from the bench by an old hog farmer who raised the boy for seventeen years. He taught the boy everything about hog farming. But the old man did evil things as well, witchcraft, devil worship and voodoo. It was found that he was killing prostitutes and feeding them to the hogs in satanic rituals. The old hog farmer rather than be arrested slit his own wrists, throat and testacies then threw himself into the hog pen. The boy took over the farm and the evil practices of the old man. Using his satanic devil worshipping skills he snatches up pimps, prostitutes, addicts and street thugs then turns them into Voodoo Negro Zombies."

"What the hell is Voodoo Negro Zombies?" I asked Cant-chance-it. "They are slaves he sends out each day to sell blood at the blood bank, turn tricks at the motel, pawn stolen property and walk around with their pants real real low being assholes. They paint and pierce their arms, legs, necks, and torso's with personal graffiti. Over perfectly blended chocolate, mocha and caramel pigment." "He's got to be bullshitting me," I said to Nubbie. "He could be, Nubbie replied, but I wouldn't chance it." "Enough of this, Nubbie he's got Rosa!"

"Go to the park behind the San Marco Library. There you'll find the Voodoo Negro Zombies."

I was out the door faster than the Supernova. Speeding past moncrief park basketball courts where lines of young black men who will never play a minute in the NBA wait their turn. Choosing to spend all day throwing a ball full of air into an empty hole, it's a shame the way the white man is holding them down.

Reaching the little one acre park was all a blur to me. It wasn't much more than a small field near the railroad tracks. Across the railroad tracks is thick undeveloped brush and trees. I saw no one as I slowly walked across the grassy field. Not until a voice from the woods told me to stop my approach, then deep in the brush I could see eyes blinking like fire flies. From the dark woods they began to appear. Their clothes were a patch work of homeless shelter chic layered three and four coats thick.

They waddled and dragged and arm or a leg with a lightening bolt scar over one eye and cockeyed in the other. A couple of dozen men and women led by a stocky built man with salt and pepper hair and beard.

"I'm HT, I lead the legion," he said.

"I'm seeking someone," I said to him.

"Who do you seek?"

"I seek the Voodoo Zombie master, Chaos, the Black Dread!" "Then you seek death." "No! I bring justice to him."

"We have seen Satan himself rise up from a crack in the earth then mark his face with a bolt of lightening during his satanic ceremony. We can escape the torture of the farm, but we're still prisoners of his existence in the world. He leads a legion of zombie warriors, HT told me."

"This jigga-boo took my boo, if I have to I'll kill them too. So tell me HT, where I might find this farm and put an end to my torture and your terror." A smile came over HT's face, "I will tell you how to find him, for my enemy's enemy is my friend".

"Where can I find his farm?"

"Take I-10 West to 301 South. You'll know you're there when you smell booty and find the crack in the road. It will point you to the Hog Farm."

With that, the bearded man led the Voodoo Negro Zombies back into the woods.

CHAPTER 26 – THE BLACK DREAD

QUICKLY RACED MY way to the Interstate 10 headed west towards State Road 301. It has moved from evening to night. It's time for the freaks to come out. The Black Dread has become a bigger than life evil villain in my mind. One thing's for sure, he done scared the fuck out of them Zombie Negroes. He must be Goliath, Cyclops and Big Foot all in one, but that don't matter. The dye has been cast and the death warrant's been printed, I said this motherfucker was going to die and I meant it.

After a ten mile ride west I reached 301 and headed south. Searching for this modern day plantation with its slaves and slave master to drench the evil fire that's burning the beauty from the soul of my city. All the while hearing Rosa's voice calling out, 'come see about me Centurion; come see about me.'

Prowling this trail marked 301 South at 27 miles per hour. My pulse rate has dropped to one beat every blink and I was hardly blinking. I have dialed down my sight, sound and feeling senses and turned up my extra sensory track a bitch down senses. I have become the steel hammer about to strike down on the cartridge to send the death bullet on its way.

Then, so quick, so quick, it came across the high way. I only caught a glimpse of it, but how could it not be the same small black helicopter I saw at a distance over my kid's soccer field in Palencia. What's it doing out here at night and barely thirty feet off the ground? I continued at my retirement community pace with my head over the steering wheel looking forward but glancing up for the helicopter.

Then, I could see a flashing light ahead on my left and was within a quarter of a mile when I saw the concrete block building with the tin roof. Within fifty yards of the matchbox structure a light over the wooden door illuminated the graffiti style words, 'Adrian's Crack in the Road Nude Bar!' In the small gravel rock parking area was another sign on a pole. On that sign was the rear of a nude woman from the waist down. Beneath the sign a light shines across the words 'Adrian's Crack in the Road Nude Bar.' The Negro Zombie told me to go to the crack in the road and I would find the Hog Farm. Across the highway is a barely noticeable road trail leading into a wooden area. I rolled the window down and I could smell it. So thick it would gag your breath. It was booty! Funky, nasty, booty! I drove about another hundred yards before I pulled my car to the side of the road between clumps of trees for camouflage. I walked around and opened the passenger door then popped open the tool box. There's hell to pay and I'm the cashier here to collect. First, I opened a can of black shoe polish then applied it to my face, neck and hands. I slid on the Kevlar vest then the double shoulder holster holding the 9 mm glocks under each arm. I buckle on my right thigh holster holding my 357 magnum, I then buckled on my left thigh holster holding my 44 magnum. I strapped onto my right ankle a small holster holding a 38 special with laser sight. Over my right shoulder, I hung the semi-automatic 45 caliber pistol. Around my waist, I fasten a double waist pouch full of hollow point, magnum and target ammo. Grabbed the shot gun then put my night vision goggles on my head. I was strapped with the full armor of God as I marched off to fight the good fight carrying enough steel, lead and gun powder to take over a small town or large Hog Farm.

I walked along the wood's edge but ducked into the thick brush when a car passed. Evil picked this fight, and then struck first, but Justice fights back. I've reached the heavily weeded, hardly noticeable one lane roadway. I flipped down the night goggles then walked the watery ditch next to the road. I felt Rosa's spirit crying out to me.

After about twenty yards of brushing off toad frogs, lizards and mosquitoes the ground began to shake and the air vibrate. A light pierced through the high weeds behind me. A car was coming from the highway with the base thumping so hard the water in the ditch rippled. I quickly lay down in the ditch. Through the weeds and horsetails I recognized the car. The same blue and white convertible with twenty inch chrome mag Rims.

It's the same sled the Albino, the African and the Black Dread road in when they killed Slick. I lifted myself for a better look. The top was down The Black Dread was sitting in the middle of the back seat. There was a long haired blonde white girl with tan skin and dark eyes driving. Standing in the front passenger seat was a brown skin black girl with titties so round they looked like pool balls. She had a waist so thin and ass so big she could only have been formed from a glass blowers pipe. She was wearing nothing but a five inch jean belt. No panties, no top, shaking booty like Trina. I could see right up her birth canal. I might have opened up the Dread's skull right then but it was dark, the car was rocking and I needed him to lead me to Rosa. Ten yards ahead they reached a six foot high wood and aluminum gate with a sign that read 'turn around and get the fuck out of here.' It opened, they entered and the gate closed behind them.

I quickly checked the safeties on my weapons making sure none where on, then climbed from the ditch and started a full sprint to the gate. I lunged and pulled myself over the top of the gate then summersault both feet to the ground and landed almost face to face with a house of a man. He had to weigh 350 pounds. No shirt, but tattoos covered his torso, Baldhead with a thick beard, smoking a cigar. "Name and rank;" I asked him? "Boss Ross, who you jigga, he responded."

"I'm the brother with the 223 pointed right at your face here to handle your funeral arrangements." "What," he asked? "Fuck it," I hit him with the hollow points. He dropped like a sundress off the shoulders of the high school scank.

I could see clearing ahead but I kept to the wooded area figuring there would be more security and I was right. A six and a half foot long drink of water was bopping to the base, carrying a bottle of gin in his right hand and a bottle of juice in his left, snooping around after hearing the big rickety house fall; I stepped from behind a pine tree as he approached. "What up, fool? What set you with?" I told him to tap his heels together three times then repeat after me. "There's no place like hell! There's no place like hell!" "Fuck you, East coast," he says. I saw two sparks come from the silencer. I dropped him with the doo-doo wop, then held it to my mouth and sucked the smoke from the barrel.

I ran another ten yards then hid behind a big palmetto pine bush. I heard someone coming. A lil' five- foot, hundred pound wheezly jigga. With tear drop tats all over his face. I jumped up and got his attention. He pulled a switch-blade. "This is a gun fight mother-fucker. Now fly away little birdie." I gave the benediction with the 45 pistol. Church was out.

I press deeper into the stink, looking to subject these black Nazi's to the poisonous gas and fire of my steal cylinders. I have made my way to the edge of the woods that reveal a large farm, probably ten acres. I never saw anything so filthy or smelt anything so bad. There was the farm house. Then next to it was a livestock barn. The blue convertible parked near the barn. I was peeking through the brush about thirty yards away. The black girl goes out on the passenger side. She was 36" 24" 44". She was why men ignore the profits and go back to Sodom and Gomorrah, in 4-inch heels looking like a Nubian Princess for real. The white chick got out then walked around to the passenger door. What you talking 'bout Hugh Hefner! Barbie doll blonde, 5'5", 115 pounds with skin the color of peach meat. Sport'n a pair of 34's that could have been custom made by Lexus. Pretty as Anna Kornikova, wearing nothing but gold open toed three inch heels and a diamond ring hanging from a piercing in her clit that's the size of a two ounce salt water fishing weight, a black berry doobie and a peach cobbler, what are they doing hanging with this road kill.

They both stood holding the door for the Black Dread. If I didn't have to kill this mother fucker, I would walk up and give him a high five.

Faster than the sound of the trigger clicking, I had become another jigga fucked because I took my eyes off the prize and had them on a piece of pussy. I spun around to a dark skinned brother who already had the drop on me. The first blast from his big silver gun hit me dead center in my chest. I fell back onto the bush. He stepped closer saying to me, "let death come, you been massacred don't fight it." As I struggled to breath, he hit me with three more shots to the chest. Then asked, "you want to rob the Dread? Well, get rich or die trying. Tonight you die!" That all sounds like some cold blooded shit, the problem for him was I'm not new to the game. I'm true to the game. I always wear the best shoes and the best Kevlar vest. The hot slugs did knock the breath out of me. However it didn't stop me from pulling my holstered 44 and 357 magnums and blowing both his arms off at the elbows. Then he pleaded; "please, give a wangster three steps!" "Run or die mother fucker!" I told him. On his third stride into the woods, I lit him up with the 223 all over the big 50 he had tattooed on his back. "That's game, set and match Centurion Justice."

The noise from the hand cannons set off a flurry of gunfire from the farm house. From behind a large tree, I could see the Black Dread firing a Mac-10 and signaling for backup as he called out "Voodoo Negro Crack Head Zombies." Around him gathered about thirty of the unhealthiest looking Voodoo Negro Crack Head Zombies you'll ever see, all of them carrying some sort of household appliance (toaster, blender, microwave, juicer, can opener) as a weapon. I was fully aware of how dangerous a crack head with a toaster could be.

Feans can be mean with their stealth physiques and lightning quick reflex ability. They are capable of throwing things long distances with incredible accuracy.

Then the Black Dread ordered the Voodoo Negro crack head zombies to attack. They sprinted towards me like they had just snatched a purse and were running for the dope house. Even with patten leather dressed shoes and two over coats them Voodoo Negro crack head zombies can scat like Deion 'prime time' Sanders. With only seconds, I remembered that crack heads although sleek are also frail. I holstered the 357 magnum and grabbed the pump shotgun hanging around my neck. I pointed and fired the shotgun. The buck shot blast sprayed the raging voodoo zombies. The lead pellets exploded the zombies like Chinese fireworks. I emerged from the bush yelling to the Black Dread, "I've come to play the killing game."

He stood there between the two Hugh Heffner's. His eyes and heart black, his mouth full of gold. His head full of nappy twisted locks, like a vulture in the midst of crows. "Well, guess who's coming to dinner?" he asked. "Girls set the table and release the hogs." The two Hugh Heffner's walked their fat ass pussys into the livestock barn.

What came from the barn was horrifying, bodies as big around as fifty five gallon drums. Every step was a five hundred pound sledge hammer hitting the earth. They were big, black and bristly. This was a hog farm and these were giant hogs. "Who-dee-who, who-dee-who," the Black Dread called out. The giant hogs began a thunderous march towards me.

No doubt they had the intention of trampling me into hog feed. But with this shotgun and 357 I'm going to change the menu. I began blasting these hog-kongs dead in the hog head cheese. The hot lead was cutting away the ham, the bacon and the pork chop. I fired round after round until the last Hog-zilla dropped in the slop.

That left only me and the Black Dread. Even the Hugh Hefner's have left. You killed my hogs but your boy squealed like a pig when we killed him at the lumber mill pit, the Black Dread yelled as I quickly approached him.

"Where is Rosa?" "Go through the hog's stomachs and you'll find what's left of her," Then the Black Dread reached into his pocket and pulled the tarot card of death, showed it to me before dropping it to the ground.

He was then surrounded by cyclone winds so strong they snatched my guns from my body and pulled the car keys from my pocket. The earth between his legs cracked. From the crack appeared a glowing light shinning only on him. His body shock and his clothes ripped, black ooze flowed from his eyes and mouth. From the pit of hell, a light illuminated this dark angel.

"Jesus, Jesus" I said and dropped to one knee.

The Black Dread proclaimed his authority. "Rulers of darkness, children of spiritual wickedness send forth your powers. From the serpent of the garden to the tower of Babble to the spirit cast into the swine to the witch and warlock. I, the zombie master, the dark lord Chaos who rains terror on Jacksonville and the world command you to rise and serve the mystical darkness." He wasn't speaking the rosary and I wasn't turning the other cheek.

Shit! It started raining again. I reached to my ankle then grabbed the only weapon I had left, the snub nose 38. I rose from my prayer position with my right arm extended and the gun pointed at the Black Dread's head. "I'm glad you can speak in tongues, I told him. It's going to come in handy when you see the Holy Ghost."

Hale Mary full of grace then the first bullet hit him in the face, just above the left eye. The next two hit him in the throat. The Black Dread fell backwards to the ground.

I walked over and stood looking down at him. With blood flowing from his forehead, mouth and throat, he still had his eyes open and gargle out the word, "Justice."

I fired one more shot into his mouth. His head snapped back and his eyes closed. "You called for Justice. Well, Justice, done come!" I began to cry and call out, "Rosa, Rosa, Rosa", then the rain stopped.

CHAPTER 27 – RAM IN THE BUSH

AFTER SURVEYING THE hog farm but only finding Rosa's shoes, blouse and Puerto Rican flag necklace, I came upon a more gruesome discovery. There was a large furnace full of burnt bones and skulls. The shock of it all left me unable to even stand on my on. The county sheriff's officer who first arrived on the scene helped me to his car. Then, assisted the medical examiner and coroners officers in documenting what they called the 'slaughter at the hog farm.'

The officer drove me to Rosa's apartment, still smelling of swamp water, hog slop, gun powder and death. I walked around in the apartment retracing all her steps. Through the kitchen and sitting in her breakfast chair while holding her coffee cup, into the living room, to the corner of the sofa where she loved to snuggle and watch lifetime television. In the bedroom, pulling back the covers to lie in her spot and press my head deep into her pillow. Going to the laundry hamper and grabbing up an armful of her panties and bras. Lord if I could taste a spoon full of her sugar again I wouldn't spill a drop and if I could hold her again I would squeeze her like a teddy bear and never let her go. It ain't over! It ain't over! It can't end like this!

I sat on the edge of the bed and cried 'till day break. The whole world cried as rain fell from the sky. With my arms still clutching Rosa's clothes, I walked from the apartment to the river bank across the street, standing on the concrete bulkhead at the edge of the water. As rain spit in my face and thunder roared in the distance. "God don't leave me here among all this sorrow and death. I must be given the opportunity to fight for the things that are beautiful and good whether they be here or in heaven."

I dropped Rosa's clothes to the ground, then my money roll, keys, black book, cell phone and the diamond ring. As Abraham lay out Jacob, I was sacrificing my first love. All that I am, I give to you Lord. I only ask that you give to me the answers that will make sense of it all and give peace to my understanding.

I stood for minutes and God never said anything. Then came my ram in the bush, through the rain and midst of the waves breaking, I could hear the faint ring of my cell phone. I picked it up and placed it to my ear. "Hello, Mr. Justice." It was Ms. Pamolis from the medical service temporary agency. "Mr. Justice, I have that file on Natalie Park's work assignments, if it can still be of assistance to you, right up to the last assignment with Dr. Sam Alldaway."

"Mr. Justice? Mr. Justice, are you there?" I was speechless. Hearing his name gave me lockjaw. Dr. Sam Alldaway was the ram in the bush!

"Mr. Justice are you still there?" Ms. Pamolis asked. "Yes," I said as my tongue broke free, "I'll be right there." I flipped the phone closed and took off running, leaving the clothes, money, keys, and black book on the ground. I was running to my car until I realized my car wasn't there. I'd left it at the hog farm and rode home with the sheriff. No cop or cab in sight. I paused in the street for a moment. How do I get there? Then from the south end of the street my answer came. I ran back to the pile of clothes and picked up my roll of money. I ran towards him as he came up the street with his black raincoat flapping in the wind.

I could only see about half of his freckled face underneath the hood of the raincoat. He looked to be about sixteen or seventeen years old pulling a homemade wagon full of newspapers on the back of his red Vespa scooter. "Young man," I yelled holding my hand up getting him to stop. "How much," I asked. "Fifty cents," he answered. "No, not the paper, the bike, how much," I asked again. "My bike," he said? "There's about ten thousand   · dollars in this roll. Count it while I un-hook this trailer." "My bike?" he asked me again. That will get you five bikes I told him as I drove off on his motor scooter. I was gunning the handle bar throttle and was ripping around corners at almost 13 mph. I weaved my way down River Road to Palm Ave. and Palm Ave to the Gary Street on ramp of the Acosta Bridge.

Up the steep on ramp, I was temped to get off and start running. It might have been faster. Nonetheless, I kept gunning it as car after car past me, over the bridge and down the exit to Park Street.

I tossed some spare change left in my pocket to the guy begging at the bottom of the bridge. Past the famous duck pond and the historic five points, a right at memorial park where the straight legged jean boys hang out. A couple of little short bulldogs came out from the park chasing me. I was able to stay just ahead of their miniature strides. It could be raining fire from the sky and I could be riding down streets flooded with gasoline, but nothing was going to stop me. Even after the city bus forced me against the curb and I hit a storm drain and fell a block away from the building. But I bounced right back up and checked to see if anyone was looking. Within minutes, I was pulling up and parking in front of the temporary medical services business. I rushed inside soaking wet. Two visitors sat in chairs to my right and Ms. Pamolis stood at the receptionist desk engaged in conversation that immediately stopped when I walked in. Ms. Pamolis held a file folder in her hand and extended it to me as I approached. "You got here fast," she said. I opened the file and flipped through it to come to Natalie's last assignment.

Well, son of a bitch, I thought. Revenge is a dish best served cold and this cold blooded bastard has been serving mine straight out the freezer box of his heart. He's done to me the most terrible thing one person can do to another, that's to wait, then get them back. "I hope that will be helpful," Ms. Pamolis said. "It's my ram in the bush," I responded. Then turned and walked towards the door. My lover and my best friend have been slain, now I find out this KKracKer's to blame.

CHAPTER 28 – SHERRIFF OF SHANGHAI

AS I EXCITED Ms Pamolis's office with the folder under my arm someone had pulled a vehicle up on the street near the scooter. A black Chevy Avalanche, part SUV and part pick-up truck with extremely dark tinted windows. As I approached the vehicle not knowing what to expect, the passenger's side window began sliding down. I was still carrying my ankle holstered 38 but if this was a hit they'd already have the drop on me.

This was no hit though. As the driver's face revealed a clean cut Asian cat with eyes of fire. "I can get you there a lot faster than that scooter," he said. "Just throw it in the back."

It was Natalie Park's (aka China Doll) brother, Michael Parks, The Sheriff of Shanghai.

I picked up the scooter and lifted it into the truck bed then got in on the passenger's side front. I hit him with a pound. We'd never met but I knew all about him. He was wearing black boots, black camouflage pants and black t-shirt with the word Police across the front. Parks was banging a Biggie Smalls–Jay Z mix tape with the base on blast. I opened the file folder to the Dr.'s name and phone number. "Who is he to you?" he asked me.

"He's the KKracKer that sent them!" He stared at the file for a moment then put the truck in drive. We pulled out, the Asian and the black, like Bruce Lee and Shaft. Michael Parks dialed the number to the doctor's office but he wasn't in. The nurse said he was out on his yacht at the King's Harbor Marina.

Parks pulled up the marina location on the GPS. He told me his street name was 'Yang-slang-lead', cause he kept the burners hot, then opened up the arm rest and revealed two 50 caliber pistols and several extra clips. We spoke a common language. He then began to speak of his sister. He spoke of her as a faithful peasant would speak of royalty for the twenty five minute drive to the Oceanside Marina. "Was that your work at the strip club on 63rd street" I asked him. "Yes it was; the strip club, the barber shop, and even the dealer around the corner from your girl Rosa." "You know where my girl lives?" "Yeah, I've seen you around. You were well ahead of me with the Albino, the African and the Black Dread". "I knew we'd eventually meet. You do good work," Parks said to me.

He then began to cry as he continued to speak 'never the righteous forsaken,' Parks proclaimed. "I feel like a black hole has opened up in my soul and sucked my life into a living hell. Nobody should live in hell alone so I'm taking these bastards with me. I branded many of them with the five pointed star and stuffed the tarot card of death in their mouth the way they did my sister and I slashed and cut their bodies into pieces to make it easier for the hell hounds to digest. They've robbed, ravaged and raped Natalie and others, now they're in the hands of the reaper. Had you met her you would know Natalie was worth more than even her weight in gold and it just wasn't going to do for anyone to say they were sorry for what they had done to her".

We had arrived in front of the private Kings Harbor Yacht ramp. Michael stopped the truck about forty yards from the guard station's huge iron gates that blocked the entrance. It was clear to us that extra precautions had been taken by someone. Instead of the usual eight dollar an hour retired coffee drinking pen pushers, there were black fatigue wearing, heavily armed brothers guarding the gate and lining the driveway.

Michael opened the arm rest and we both pulled a 50 caliber and extra clips. "You ever think about dying?" he asked me. I paused to think for a moment, then answered, "If you're never really afraid then you never actually die." Michael Parks smiled then he smashed the accelerator to the floor. Crashing threw the towering gates like nine eleven. Surprising them with the shock and awe, driving hard 'til we stood on the bow of the boat and proclaimed mission accomplished. Armed urban mercenaries are springing up from behind dumpster caves and out of cardboard fox holes like the Taliban.

BOOM! BOOM! BOOM! He fired three shots and turned to run. BOOM! BOOM! I fired and hit him in the back and saw him cough up a lung. They're lining the driveway all strapped with a gun, I'm blasting that magnum steel taking out two for one. One's on the right, one's on the left, one's holding 9's on each hip, the others gripping a mach 10 and got extra clips. NO matter their weapons their fates have been sealed. Two jet eye jiggaz got blood to spill, got the 50 calibers out the window on rapid recoil. Both barrels hot, Red beam aimed right at their sweet spot. When they ask you who shot you, you can tell them both jiggaz got you!

They're throwing up nines and shootin' nine times. I'm shootin' once and taking all their nine lives. My manz behind the wheel is zig zagging all crazy like he was high on that leaf. That 12 cylinder front wheel drive Chevy's charging hard up into Dr. Sammy's fortress. The way they're blasting back you'd think they were protecting Bin Laden and we were the U.S. government. Although just like Uncle Sam hunting the Saudi, I'm after the KKracKer that sent the shorties.

At the end of the pavement behind a high voltage security fence is the concrete dock leading up to the 190 foot yacht. Word is true, we do fight against powers, principalities and evil in high places. Standing in front of the fence about 5'9" tall and 140 pounds, looking like a pig with lipstick and wearing snake berry colored leather vest and jeans is a muscular, tattooed, pierced up GI Jane. Gripping a chain in her left hand that's holding an Alaskan Snow dog and a Rottweiler with an AK-47 in her right, she got the barrel sparking like she was fighting off the Russians from the waters of Wasilla. She was going straight rogue unleashing a hail of full metal jackets on the truck's grill and hood. Between the sounds of metal splitting metal, the Chinese brother asked me my policy on handling women. I told him, "I got 99 problems but a bitch ain't one, you tag her and I'll bag her." He leaned harder on the pedal and made all the bitches' hood ornaments as we smashed through the fence and up the ramp to the big boat.

We went airborne, soaring through the air like a black B-52 bomber. Still dropping atomic lead on these ghetto bammers, we flew over the mysterious black Mercedes parked at the end of the ramp and crashed into the little black helicopter sitting on the pad at the rear of the ship. So did the facts come crashing through my mind. The black Mercedes, the little black helicopter, the Albino, the African and the Black Dread were all wasp from the same nest.

The 'copter, the dogs and the bitch went over the side and into the water. The truck came to rest on the pad. Shanghai Parks sprung from the truck among a blaze of gun fire. He leapt from position to position like a cat on a hot tin roof. I loaded another clip into the 50 caliber pistol and jumped out the passenger door. From behind the truck with the 50 in my left hand, I reached down and took the 38 short from the holster of my right ankle. I then laid down cover fire for Parks, as the gunfire was coming from a half dozen or so long dreaded Rasta' types.

Make murder, rude boy! Make murder!" I heard one yelling. Bullets flying all around his head from murderous black dreads still ain't nobody chiller, that boy Parks is as cool as the other side of the pillow.

With Park's ancient kung-fu and my expert high caliber gun work, we were able to rapture these Bob Marley's to a marijuana field high in the sky. Once I blasted the last one's hemp weave, I surveyed the bullet riddle upper deck of the three level mega Yacht. Stepping over dead dreads and marveling at this jewel of a vessel with the finest wood, linen and gold fixtures. I know little about marine design but I know million dollar décor whether it be land, sea or air. Boats and Benz's, Helicopter and hit men, this KKracKer paid but I'm here to make sure he gets paid back. I be damned if it didn't start to rain again.

That's when I heard the gunfire from the lower deck and my tour of the fabulous life of Dr. Sammy was over. The opulence of the upper cabins was gone once I descended the staircase to the lower level. I had entered a cavern of gothic darkness with black and purple carpet, furniture and walls, blacked out windows with light only coming from black candles on tables and counter tops. The smoke smell of incents filled the room. There were pentagrams, half-moon symbols, tarot cards and books on witchcraft throughout the large open cabin. Chained to a steel pole in the center of the room is a large iguana lizard. I moved slowly and carefully like a person whose shoes were tied way to tight.

Both guns drawn, I approach a hallway at the end of the room and there I find Kong-fu Parks lying on his back with a torso full of bullet holes. Slightly conscious and barely breathing, I knelt over his seeping body. "Gon see my sister. Gon see my sister," he whispered. "Yeah, that's right, I said to him, you are going to see your sister." "You saved, brother?" I asked him. "I'm Buddhist", he mumbled. "Will you accept Jesus Christ as your Lord and Savior?" I asked him. "Sure," Parks responded. "Then you're saved and you'll see your sister again." "Thanks, so are you going to save the doc too?" Parks asked me. "Well, for everyone I save I send 666 to hell and I ain't met my quota yet." An easy peace came over him, then in the twinkling of an eye he was gone to see his sister.

I took a deep gulp and swallowed the large piece of vengeance life had just served me. This Kkracker's barrel had served up death to the Sheriff of Shanghai, be careful Centurion.

CHAPTER 29 – THE KKRACKER THAT SENT HIM

DETERMINED, I WOULD pursue my enemy even deep into the pits of hell.

I stood and continued through the hallway to a large suite, with a toilet, walk-in shower, a vanity, love seat and sliding glass doors that opened to the bow of the ship. Then as I turned to my left, I gasped in horror as I see Rosa's nude body spread eagle and face up on a queen sized bed. I rush to the right side of the bed placing the guns on the floor to check her vital signs.

"Rosa! Rosa! Rosa!" I called her name as I brushed her curly black hair back from her face. Why was she here? I thought she had been killed at the hog farm. I gently held her left wrist and put my ear to her chest checking for a heart beat or a pulse. There was none. The glory chariot was filling up.

I rested my head in the pit of her neck and spoke into her ear. "I will see you again, Rosa. I will see you again. I will search the heavenly kingdom and I will find you. I will see you again." With every blink my eyes would sprinkle her with a tear. Lord, I want my baby back. The folding door of the closest at the foot of the bed sprang open and there was Dr. Sammy.

Standing about 6'5" with sun burnt skin about thirty five years old. His hair was white blonde and his eyes were extremely blue. With his gun drawn down on me, "Don't you move," he said. "How did she get here?" I asked him. "I was able to get her off the hog farm just before you turned it into a pork processing plant." I then remembered the helicopter passing low as I made my approach. My shoulders and head sank as I realized I might have saved her had I been minutes earlier.

"You're going to pay dearly for this," I told the doc. "Two things will get you fucked up, fucking the wrong woman or fucking with the wrong dude. You did both and in case you're wondering, she suffered mightily as I choked the life out of her. That is after I had her held down and I ate her guts up for an hour and a half. I don't think I need to tell you; that is good eating." "This honky was hitting my hate bone."

"My life flowed into hers like a creek stream into a river, I responded. At this moment you've left me a muddy ditch." "I still can't get my lip to stop quivering", Dr. Sammy said with a half smile. Me being well verse in street provocation, I held quick my reaction to his revelation of desecrating Rosa's body. We paused and stared into each other's soul. Our eyes like dueling laser beams.

"You think I knew fucking this white woman would cause me this much misery and pain. Now I know all pussy's pink but it ain't all the same. I ain't got to tell you white pussy ain't all that, if you really want something sweet take a bite of that chocolate kit kat. I'm a better man today than I was before all this misery began, I told the Dr. It's unfortunate, because you're never going to know any of my new found goodness. My spirit say's you're guilty of unforgiveable sin and Jesus wants you dead. So consider this your home going ceremony cause I'm gonna kill you deader than dead, but first I must know. Why Slick and Rosa? Why did they have to die?"

"Because, the Dr. yelled, you weren't there when the Dread, African and Albino came to kill you. If I couldn't get you, I would get those nearest and dearest to you. I'd do to you what you did to me. I'd take from you what you took from me."

"But why Natalie Parks then? It's unimaginable that human beings would carry out such a horrendous act. Why?" I asked Dr. Sammy again. "I'll tell you why. The Medical Temp Agency said she would be thorough. She was…she was too thorough. She stumbled across my private payout books." "You took her life in such a horrific way because of some phony books?" I asked him. "This was my life we're talking here. This boat, the house, the cars and helicopter, you think I got all this from operating on people's feet and doing part time work for a football team. She came across the listings of all the illegal aliens I was supplying social security numbers and fraudulent medical claims. Not just the coffee, but the women, the house, the boat and the bodyguards. All take cream or cheddar, or bankroll, or filthy luger, or whatever you people want to call it and she was going to report it. So, I sent the Black Dread and his Voodoo Zombie Negroes out to cancel her claim."

"You sent this plague on her to protect your boy toys and you killed my loved ones because I fucked your woman? I didn't pull her, she pulled me! You KKracKers always say it's about the Economy, that it's about your kids future, that it's about family, country and patriotism but it's about one thing and one thing only! The three inch slit and the nine inch barrel, your people's pussy and my people's dicks, you've always been scared as fuck about a brother like me getting your woman in the buck! I paid for this with my career, my family and my future," I screamed back at Dr. Sammy.

"Stop trippin' on your own self" Dr. Sammy yelled back. His hand trembling as he pointed his gun square at me. "This wasn't about fucking a jigga! he said, you people are so full of yourself, with your basketball, your football, your Tiger Woods and your hip-hop dancing, yall ain't leaving no white pussy for our kids and grandkids and with Obama creating this deficit little white boys won't be able to buy any pussy."

"Dr Sammy I ain't try'n to claim your shit, you think I want to wake up one day in a bed with an old white woman and a house full of shih tzus. Don't be crazy, I just wanted a nut, little did I know your ass was fucking nuts."

Then with his right arm still aiming his pistol at me he unbuttoned and zipped down his khaki jeans with his left hand. "Now, now you know! Dr. Sammy said shaking his gun in front of me. You know why I love big toys." It was incredible. I could barely keep from staring at it. It could easily be the ninth wonder of the world. On a full grown man no less, not as big a Vienna sausage. It was the size of a boiled peanut. It was the dick he was born with and it hadn't changed or grown one bit. He could fill up Allison's purse, but not her panties. "Why do you think I had all this satanic shit around? I tried every Voodoo doctor, Devil worshipper and Witch in town to get this dick to grow. I've tried every witch's potion and eaten everything from raccoon to hog nuts. This bitch won't get one inch longer or one centimeter thicker. I was about to eat that iguana before you busted in."

"Why do you think all these blacks are around here. Every jigga and his play cousin was tappin' Allison's ass with their big dicks. Then you came along and killed her. You killed my blond goddess, vexed my soul and stole the jewel from my throne. You no driving some bitch, you killed her and totaled my new car. The Black Dread was supposed to put a curse on you and have fire and brimstone rain on your head whenever you came near any of us. But all that voodoo Negro did was make it rain, they got fucked up and you just got wet. Just like the car crash someone was watching over you. But not even Jesus from his throne can stop me from killing you and I'll still get to Paradise. I stole my way here I'll steal my way there."

"It was an accident," I said. "Accident my ass, she was the most beautiful flower I'd ever picked and she understood my handicap. You know how many women will make fun and ridicule you for a baby dick?" "I wouldn't know nothing about that", I answered the doc. He looked hard at me with his steel blue eyes as he zipped his pants. Then as I saw the tendons in his arm start to tighten he said, "You, you my friend have been the architect of your own doom and today is your doomsday."

I stood from the bed and began to back up towards the night stand. "Wait a minute," I said hoping to buy myself time to think. Then like they say at the holiness church, I opened my mouth to let the spirit speak, verbally attacking this KKracKer like I was high on cotton gin.

"Men like you always blame men like me, but you know it's not true. You know it's always a KKracKer like you, through your greed, lust, impatience and indifference unleashes a jigga. But you know all along how dangerous the jigga is. You know material lust, low intellects, gold teeth and gun powder don't mix".

"You know you never should have brought that jigga here. You know you never should have set that jigga free. You know you never should have moved from the school house steps and let that jigga in. You knew not to elect that beautiful black man President. Even though your daddy got a baby by his kin you still can't let that jigga win".

"For four hundred years you've been riding our backs but even after Harvard and hale to the Black you won't even cut Obama no slack, but don't you come at him wack, because forty million black got that jigga's back."

"A klan of KKracKers and some rich black folks held a biracial caucus on how to kill the Kenyon, I know you're smart but I ain't retarded, to the best of my recollection that's how that slavery shit got started".

"Here you go following that new Jim Crow; Hannity, O'Reilly, Beck, Limbaugh and Joe: can we please impeach that jigga and elect a more light skinned figure, oh I know, how about them stooges (Curly, Larry, Palin or Moe) Palin! You KKracKers must have lost your mother fucking mind, your momma must have drop you on your head. He won the primary you bought a big knife, he won the nomination you bought a big pistol, he won it all you bought a big riffle, they swore him in you killed your wife, killed your kids, killed your dog, killed your mother-in-law, killed the milk man, then said you were on a mission to stop that Murdering Marxist Motherfucking Muslim. Every vampire in Twilight was white, yet you tremble in fear over this one brother from the Chi-lights.""

"You use words like patriots, real Americans and regular folks instead of a hood with the eyes cut out. The rope and the gun, the tar and the feathers, secrets you'll never tell, till you get to hell. You're always crying about being broke; the countries broke, big business is broke, small business is broke, you're broke, but we spent all our money buying your shit. Your houses, cars and insurance, what did you do with all that money? Loose it at the dog track! I know Caca ain't got it, I just saw that motherfucker riding a bicycle down the street, stop that crying bitch before my mama gets her belt. I mailed you my tithes and offerings but when those Klux came and burnt my house down you wouldn't throw me a Bottle of water. Someone call the Black phone in the oval office and tell them to go to Plan B; have the jiggaz we don't want join the Tea Party, breed with their daughters and turn them all into Creoles."

"Whinny bitches, you say you don't believe in abortion until your daughter brings that jigga home to meet the proud grandparents then you run to the closet to get a clothes hanger. Cowardly bastard shoot an unarmed family planning doctor in the back at church, even Jessie James told a man to draw first. We don't like the way this Country's going, who the fuck is "we" and how come "we" all white!"

"Twelve hundred dollar pin stripped suites cover your scarlet letter written with the blood of Emmett Till, Martin Luther King and Medger Evers. You've shown no affirmative action and took away all that was set aside, but the Asians own your money and banks, the Arabs own your land and oil, India owns your technology, a jigga don't own shit but you hate his fucking guts".

"I can pull myself up by my boot straps if you will cut down this noose from around my neck. We worked your forty acres on your mule then at the end of the day you charged us for bread and water and said it was the conservative right Christian thing to pay. No credit for a jigga, no loan for a jigga, no job for a jigga but read the paper, now you know you reap what you sow".

"You enslaved our ballers with your daughters and your MTV cribs, that whoe was crazy from the get go. From Tyson to Kobe, she said she was his biggest fan, that's why she gave him the clap then spent all his money and left him with crap. Ask Hercules, Sampson and all the Titans, they use to throw deep now their shot dead in their sleep."

"We fought our dogs, you locked us up. We shoot ourselves in the leg, you lock us up. If you don't want to pay us we don't give a fuck, but your son's got all our autographed players cards don't leave us on stuck!"

"You told people some of your best friends were black but from M.J. to Eldridge you gave up that booty then took them for millions. I need you to do me a huge favor, and suck my dick! Damn right I said it, put your head in my lap and give me a Malkin. I got your rehab, just put your hand in my front right pocket. A Tiger is suppose to hunt and devour prey. Don't let these KKracKers tame you boo, before they're done you'll be in a zoo."

"We let go our pride and character, the secret to our strength and you unleashed Michlilah Steele and the Black Republistines then invited us to a Tea Party to lynch our ass. Hey Newt! That god damn Billy Bob forgot the hoods and the sheets. Fuck that, leave the rope and take the riffles, we'll just call ourselves a militia."

"All the while yelling 'give me my Country back', it was never your Country bitch! You stopped by for Thanksgiving dinner and while the Chief was watching the game and sleeping off his turkey you were in the back fucking his squaw and forging the deed. You stole people's property from the Persian Gulf to Pandora."

"Fuck you jigga! Dr Sammy screamed, you don't scare me just because you get hype."

"Damn right I'm hyped," I answered the Doctor. "I'm hyped and I'm amped, most of my heroes don't appear on no stamp, Glen Beck is a hero to most KKracKers but he don't mean shit to me. A straight up racist, the sucker is simple and plain, mother fuck him, Rush Limbaugh, Sean Hannity and John McCain".

"You've been the ultimate American Gangster. A jigga may be the symptom, but it's the KKracKer that sent him that's the disease!"

CHAPTER 30 – THE JUDAS AND JESUS'S HITMAN

I LOOKED FOR A response from Dr. Sammy, after I had talked about everything but his mammy, but the bullet down the barrel was all I could see, this KKracKer was about to kill me! His skin turned red from the bottom of his neck to the top of his head. Rage rushed across his face and all I heard was just one word, "NIGGAAAAAAAAAAAAAAAAAAAAA!!!"

In my spirit I had claimed victory, but there was no time to get a gun in my hand. I drew the phone book from the night stand, slung it to my face as hollow points blasted yellow pages all over the place. I opened the book and lunged towards him, slamming the gun in the book. The gun fired piercing the binding and striking my left shoulder. He kept dropping the hammer till every chamber was empty, with my shoulder stinging and blood spilling. We twirled and spun like two gays dancing with the stars.

This white dude wasn't no snow flake though. He was cock strong and his wind was long. We crashed through the sliding glass doors onto the lower level bow of the ship, knocking over the fabulous chic designer furniture. Armed with a strong hold and evil intentions this KKracKer threw me from side to side of the ship's bow until I was nearly sea sick. I still wouldn't let him go.

Choking, scratching, punching and kicking, we hit the railing then fell from the yacht splashing into the Atlantic like synchronized belly floppers, him pulling me down like Tavis does Barack. Pass lobsters and crab, through schools of red snapper and drum, we tumbled and tussled all the way to the Ocean's bottom. I never loosened my grip on him. Knowing if I kept squeezing, I'll get him like white folk got O.J.

He clawed at my arms as my hands gripped him tighter. Digging his fingernails into my skin while trying to kick me off of him, I could feel him weakening. His eyes bugged and his blue contact lenses popped out. His body began to quiver. His lips moved as if to form the word, 'please.' What? KKracKer please!

I see his life is leaving him but I still can't let him go. I felt myself suffocating from the lack of oxygen. Numbness began to move through my body. I could no longer hold my breath. I could feel the millions of cells throughout my body bursting a hundred at a time. My vision began to flicker on and off 'till it was no more than a tunnel of white light leading to even brighter light. I not only released his body, but released mine also. I felt myself blast off up the tunnel of light like a rocket ship. Faster than the day break. Was this death or was this life multiplied by its highest power. The light purified my being as it purged me of all transgression. It stripped away my adultery, my fornication, my covetousness, my lies, my murders, my idolatry and my false witness. I burst from the light and landed on my knees on the streets of glory.

All the profits and all the revelations were true, streets of gold, emeralds, diamonds and rubies. No sun, just the heavenly glow. Along the road was a stream of milk and honey leading up to an enormous gate. Behind the gate were magnificent mansions and castles that rose higher than I could see. I rose to my feet and began to walk towards the gate in my new perfectly constructed eternal body, wearing gold sandals, white silk baggy pants and a white knee length silk robe with no shirt. Just before the gate on my right was a huge throne, a great throne, a magnificent throne of jewels, gold and marble.

Standing next to the throne was a young man wearing only a loin cloth and sandals. He was twirling a sling shot around his fingers and playing with the little button eyed puppy from the pit. On the opposite side of the throne stood a large white horse, on top the horse sat a man covered in a crimson colored robe and hood. I could not see his face, but his eyes of fire shined bright out of the hood's darkness. On the throne 'He' sat. King of kings, Prince of peace, the Son!

He wore a full length white robe trimmed in gold. He's rocking a Jackson five afro with a goatee like the one Ike Turner had when he was with Tina. Both were white as lamb's wool. His face was narrow like Prince and his eyes were a kaleidoscope of colors. Sitting on the right arm rest of the throne wearing a two piece cream colored see through silk halter top and mini skirt, in her perfected body, looking like Appolonia, pointing at me while she whispered in his ear, is Rosa; for every King a Kingdom, for every Kingdom a Queen.

At his feet with her left arm wrapped around his calf and her head resting on his lap is China Doll, the Afro-Asian princess. Her body raptured to new, she's dressed in white too.

To my left was a river of crystal colored water. Standing on the water's surface were legions of young blonde warriors. Faces like Brad Pitt, bodies like mix martial arts fighters, all strapped with bow and arrows. Their heads bowed towards the throne. I stand at the throne and look up at him.

That's a pretty ass brother! He looked hard at me, but did not speak. As I turn to look away from the truth and life which beamed from his being. I saw the heavenly Choir marching into the gate, one line from the right, the other on the left. Being directed by Michael Jackson who was singing lead to a Kirk Franklin praise song, that brother still Bad!!!

To the left it was him! Just as he said he would, Dr. Sammy had stolen his way to the end of the line entering the large gate to the holy city. I strained to get the words out. "There's a Judas in the midst," I said.

Hanging from the left arm of the throne was a white bow and a cache of silver arrows. The Lamb of God took the bow from the arm rest and an arrow from the cache and handed them to me. He said nothing but I understood every word. I positioned the arrow in the bow and raised it to my head to take aim. As I placed my eye to the arrow, I noticed an inscription on the tail fin; 'J.C.' Doctor Sammy was just steps from entering the gate when I let the arrow go. It left my hand with a sound like a bullet shot from a silencer. He turned the corner and the arrow hit the gate post. All the prayers Christ has answered for me and he only asked me to kill this KKracKer and I missed. Before I could ask myself What Would Jesus Do, his arm raised with finger pointed to the Gate, "Go get that blue eyed Judas", he ordered.

I took off after him. With every step my eternal senses traced his movement, from Lucifer to Satan, Satan to Beelzebub, Beelzebub to Mephistopheles, Mephistopheles to the Devil, the Devil to the Anti-Christ, the Anti-Christ to the KkracKer that sent him.

Through the gate I entered the garden. He turned into a serpent and slithered along the ground. I ran to the only tree in the middle of this eve's paradise then broke off a branch. I chased the serpent through strawberry fields in the midst of a purple haze. Strike after strike but never a hit. From the garden he stood and ran as a man down a rocky mountain side into the parted sea. I chased him just ahead of the Pharaohs chariots to the sound of freed slaves singing Black Mose's, I stand accused, Isaac Hayes on base. He leaped time and space emerging as a mothers temptress dancing for the head of the Baptist. I crashed the party then broke up the band. I lunged for her weave. She slipped my grasp as thirty pieces of gold. That gold was toll for a snitch named Judas in the greatest story ever told. Through history we raced, all along the way he tried to destroy my race. He couldn't shake me; he disguised himself but couldn't fake me.

When he couldn't lose me he tried hiding in the right wing of the kingdom. This evil arch angel I must subdue before he converts others to his point of view. I gathered four of glory's gate keepers; Martin, Malcolm, Medgar and Slick. Jesus ordered me to solve this case so I took his guards and bum-rushed the place. We found him making sculptures of himself and calling it the Christ. With thin lips, straight hair, blue eyes, I'm glad I caught him before he spreaded them lies.

"Why do you relentlessly pursue me, Dr Sammy said, in this kingdom there's no price on my head."

"You're wrong, you have taken innocent lives, I said, Centurion Justice is Jesus' Hit man` and Jesus wants you dead!"

"Please grant one last reguest of an evil retch, Dr Sammy pleaded. May I have a drink of the cool living water that flows so freely here for God's sons and daughters?" "I'll do for you what in life you would not do for Slick, China Doll and Rosa. I will show mercy. I'll grant a last request of the evil and retched, but I want get it, you step your ass up and fetch it."

"What do you want done with him," Martin asked. "Take him to the mountain top for final judgment", I replied. "How do you want it done", Malcolm asked. "By any means necessary", I answered. He was bound in all his deceit, enslavement, rapes and murders then taken to be thrown in the lake of fire.

"Any last words" Slick asked. As they took him away, I looked into his extremely blue eyes and said; "From the ghetto to glory, you do dirt, Justice gone get you."

I went back to the throne. The Prince of Peace stepped down from his seat. Looking at me with no expression, his eyes forced me to look up at him. He's much taller in person. He then spoke to me with the voice of supreme authority, "You've killed him in life! Now, you've killed him in death! Go back, it's not your time.

You've fought savages and wild beast, dangerous creatures, witches and warlords on the way to the throne. What a life you have lived, a life I've never known. To battle your way to the foot of the throne and its true riches of wisdom and truth, love and faith, now take these jewels and go.

I sit high and look low, the world is my footstool. When I walked on ground them KKracKers ordered me dead and them jigga's killed me. Kill me once and get away with it then shame on you, kill my sisters and brothers and get away with it then shame on me.

Armageddon comes later, first comes Justice."

"But Lord so many times I fell."

"You stumbled but never fell, he said, the light of my love always shined over you."

"Why couldn't I see you?"

"I was the seat belt in the car crash with Allison Alldaway, I was Rosa when you needed refuge; I was the puppy barking at the lumber mill pits. I was the wooden spike at the wood pile when you faced the Albino; I was the car passing during the shootout at Kandi's. I was the little Bible in your pocket at the alligator farm when you faced the African; I was the 38 special around your ankle when you faced the Black Dread. I was the phone book on the Dr's boat. I have always been with you and deep down you've always known it. Besides that you kept calling my name and if you lift me up I'll pull you up, how else do you think you got here? I've sent an invitation to all the brothers and sisters but they've ignored my words and would not answer my call."

"Yes Lord and now I'm ashamed, I have followed the flesh, I said to the King of Kings. I did bad things without repentance, I have fucked some of the baddest broads, I killed some of the baddest men, wore some of the baddest clothes and drove some of the baddest rides." "Yes you did, even when your life was crap I stood in the gap. My grace is sufficient and victory is in my name not yours. When you called my name I made you my brother and if you're my brother I've got your back."

"Those who have forged my name spring from their Fox hole stealing what is right then with a smile say I blessed them, their liars. It was a jack and I want it back!"

"I will not forgive nor forget the murders of innocent women and children, good men and women, unarmed persons during a robbery, killing for any racial reason or because someone doesn't believe in your political, religious or social views. I find you innocent of these things".

"Now go fight for me, the kingdom is at hand but it must be taken violently. So I need real soldiers that will love their community, raise their children, treat a good woman right, walk like a God, won't bow to the man and take a high from his hand, doing wrong in the dark then in the light proclaiming themselves the right. To hell with evil bidders and two faced whinny beggars".

"I said on the Cross I would live again and so will you! I bled so you wouldn't have to. I died so you could live".

"But Lord how can I repay you?"

"There are things in the world I cannot stand but I don't want evil men's blood on my hands, I need you to be my Hit man".

"Lord say the word I'll do all I can, even if it means killing a man".

"Seldom have I found such faith in all the world Centurion. Always remember when your days get dark and you find yourself looking down the barrel of a gun, don't you run, just hala at the Son. Now go, there's more to be done!"

"Jesus you are Lord but what will you tell 'the Father'."

"I will tell him, I called for Justice and Justice done come, Centurion Justice."

I turned and walked back towards the light.

THE END

Kind of

Grimy to Glorious, Sinner to Sanctified, and all the explicit details in between

Thanks to:
Edward Keyes, Model
Steve Hiday, Photographer
Prem Devi Dahl Pride, Picture Editor